GW00775855

A DEATH IN THE WEDDING PARTY

1911. Love is in the air. Despite an unfortunate resemblance to her horse, Lady Richenda Stapleford has accepted an offer of marriage. Euphemia too has accepted one of her beaux. But the course of true love does not run true for upstairs or downstairs. Euphemia, the estranged granddaughter of an Earl, who launched her career as a maid in the household of the corrupt MP Lord Stapleford has now risen to the rank of housekeeper. When a senior member of the wedding party is murdered it falls to Euphemia to solve the crime.

WITHDRAWN FROM STOCK

A DEATH IN
THE WEDDING PARTY

A Death In The Wedding Party

by

Caroline Dunford

Magna Large Print Books
Long Preston, North Yorkshire,
BD23 4ND, England.

British Library Cataloguing in Publication Data.

A catalogue record of this book is
available from the British Library

ISBN   978-0-7505-4428-3

First published in Great Britain by Accent Press Ltd. 2013

Copyright © Caroline Dunford 2013

Cover illustration © Accent Press

The right of Caroline Dunford to be identified as the author of this
work has been asserted by her in accordance with the Copyright,
Designs and Patents Act, 1988

Published in Large Print 2017 by arrangement with Accent Press

All rights reserved. No part of this publication may be reproduced,
stored in a retrieval system, or transmitted in any form or by any
means, electronic, mechanical, photocopying, recording or otherwise
without the prior permission of the Copyright owner.

Magna Large Print is an imprint of Library Magna Books Ltd.

Printed and bound in Great Britain by
T.J. (International) Ltd., Cornwall, PL28 8RW

The story contained within this book is a work of fiction. Names and characters are the product of the author's imagination and any resemblance to actual persons, living or dead, is entirely coincidental.

Fingal County Libraries

Chapter One

A Proposal

'Yes! Oh yes, my darling!'

The golden sunset streamed through the open door, casting long shadows across the black-and-white-squared hallway floor. It touched the head of the ecstatic woman, crowning her with fire and showing her complexion in the best possible colour. Discreet shadows hid all sign of blemishes in this perfect moment.

The man wore a dark suit; a charming figure of mystery and promise. A faint aroma of the flower-beds permeated Stapleford Hall. Really, the setting could not have been more romantic for a proposal. The man arose from one knee as the lady launched herself at him. Unfortunately the delighted young lady was the slightly larger of the two. They collapsed in an undignified heap.

I moved quietly behind a column, but not so far I could not still peek my face around the side and watch the drama, or rather the tangle of arms and legs, unfolding. Lady Richenda Stapleford, only daughter of the house, would be livid if she knew I had witnessed her fall.

'Dash it, Richenda! You might let a man get the ground underneath himself before you charge like a bull at a gate.'

9

'Oh Tippy, darling. I'm so sorry. I'm just a teensy-weensy bit over excited.'

'I should bally say. There was I expecting your butler to open the door and dash me if you don't open the bally thing yourself and then demand, yes demand, what I have to say to you.'

'But you rang and said you had something urgent to say to me.'

'Yes, but I was hoping to say it in the drawing room or even the library. Somewhere a man could conduct himself with a little decency and decorum. And not,' he turned round to look out the open door, 'with half the county gawping at me. Honestly, Rich, it doesn't do. Doesn't do at all!'

'Oh, Tippy, you don't mean to say you don't mean it?'

Baggy Tipton disentangled himself, got to his feet and smoothed down his already slick hair. One greasy strand flopped disobediently over his best feature, his electric blue eyes. He did not look happy. Lady Richenda Stapleford also got to her feet – floundered might be a more accurate description. Her swain did not offer a hand, and the quantity of fabric a dress fit to be proposed in had demanded was excessive even by her own unique standards.

Her long red hair scattered hairpins pitter-pat across the tiled floor. She was breathing heavily from the situation and her exertions. In fact, considering her unfortunate propensity to look like a horse, one could almost say she was snorting; her wide nostrils flaring. I was sure it was far from the scene either of them had envisaged. Was this engagement about to end as soon as it had started? My sole interest in the outcome, other than comical purposes, was to know whether I might soon be deprived of Richenda. Since I had tried, unsuccessfully, to have her elder brother committed for the murder of their father, and that time she had locked me in a cupboard, we had not been the best of house companions.

Out of the corner of my eye I glimpsed a small movement. Across from me, also partially hidden behind a pillar was the butler, Rory McLeod, who had obviously been on his way to answer the door before Lady Richenda pre-empted him. I caught his eye willing him to share a smile with me at this farcical scene, but the face turned towards me was cold as stone.

But then I suppose when you have told a man you would rather remain in service as a house-keeper to a suspected murderer than marry him, it is unlikely he will share a joke with you, or even, to be fair, share the time of day.

The life of a servant is a life spent being invisible, coming in halfway through conversations and events and ignoring them. We must leave our betters to their own business. Even when our betters are murderers, thieves, liars and dealers in weapons of destruction. Or that is what Rory would say in his lovely Scotch burr. Of course I could remind him of the time that his 'betters' had accused him of murder and been all ready to lynch him if it hadn't been for my interference. I could further avow the black-heartedness of a family where the eldest son had killed his father, except Rory had not been present for that episode and

11

the only other person who knew undoubtedly of his guilt was his younger brother, Bertram. Bertram had also asked me to marry him, despite the all too recent loss of his previous love, and again I had declined, preferring instead to work for his – not to mince words – evil half-brother. Not surprisingly, he wasn't on speaking terms with me either.

From the above you will have gathered I am not a very good servant. I stick my nose in where it should not be. I question, I observe and I act on my intuition much to everyone's disgust. Lord Stapleford promoted me to the position of house-keeper, I am sure, to keep an eye on me. He would rather have me here than stirring up trouble now I have contacts with the OS, part of our British In-telligence service, than loose to cause real trouble. Though I suppose to be honest it is more accurate to say the OS have used me. Sir Richard Stapleford is a man of means with his own bank, his armaments business and now he is a rising star in the House of Commons. The intelligence services seem to share my view he is generally an all-round bad egg, but apparently it is not easy to clap up a peer of the realm, who is also an MP. It is also not easy to walk away from an entanglement with this man's life and in so doing retain your own. For example, much as I have been enjoying the nuptial farce in the hallway, I am almost certain it is the seemingly harmless joker, Baggy Tipton, who killed my predecessor, Mrs Wilson. Heavens, you are no doubt thinking, this girl should run far, far away. She must be a complete idiot to stay. Believe me, there are days when I would agree with you.

But my father, the Reverend Joshua Martins, handicapped me with a strict sense of right and wrong, a passion for justice and, much to my mother's lament, the ability to use my intellect. Sadly, however, he did not leave us provided for and when he expired most suddenly in his dish of mutton and onions, mother, myself and my little brother Joe, found ourselves on the brink of destitution. Once more my mother appealed to my grandfather, who is an Earl, and once again he ignored her. My mother had married far below her station and for love. Reality and poverty had destroyed that illusion. Now, mother is partially supported by my wage and also teaches piano in a small village. It is enough for us to hope we may be able to save to send little Joe to school when he is ten. Little Joe is not keen on this idea at all, but both mother and I are determined to give him the chance to have some small part of the life his grandfather has denied him.

Of course, no one at Stapleford Hall has the faintest idea that I outrank all of them, and my mother has no idea that my dearest friend is Merry, the senior maid. If this all seems topsy-turvy to you, then I ask you to take a look around yourself. The world is in chaos. It is 1911. We have had the hottest summer on record. The heat appears to have entered the brains of my fellow countrymen. There has been the most terrible civil unrest. A Latvian crime gang held a shoot-out in our capital city! The Liverpool transport workers clashed with police in what shall for ever be known as Bloody Sunday. The only glimpse of joy through the riots has been the June coro-

13

nation of King George V and Queen Mary. Though I have to say Queen Mary looks most formidable. If anyone could get this nation into shape I imagine she could. The less said about her husband's partying lifestyle, the better.

There is much more I could tell you, but you now have the gist of things: I am of the wrong station for my position; I have mortally offended the two most important men in my life; my employer is an evil man who gets away with evil deeds and I am a vicar's daughter, who still hopes to find incontrovertible evidence of the misdemeanours of her employer. The late housekeeper, Mrs Wilson, said she had papers that would reveal all. Part of the reason I took the position was to find them. I have not been successful. Nothing is right in the world.

The heavy steps of Lord Stapleford interrupted my revelries. I judged it was more than time for me to slip back below stairs. Rory, I noted, had already disappeared in a breath of butler-ish decorum.

Downstairs Mrs Deighton was preparing dinner.

'Tell me they're all set to sit down,' said the harassed cook, 'only one more minute and these pigeon breasts will turn to dust.'

I gave Mrs Deighton a look. 'Ooooh, no, Euphemia,' she cried, sinking down on a stool and throwing her apron over her head. 'What have they done now?'

When the cook notices more than her dinner you know a household has really gone to seed. 'It is a happy occasion,' I said calmly. 'It would appear that Lady Richenda has accepted the hand

14

of the honourable Mr Tipton in marriage.'

Merry, who had been good naturedly helping out our new scullery maid, went into whoops of laughter. The butler entered the kitchen.

'I see no reason for mirth,' said Rory, 'beyond some lamentably soft carrots, Mrs Deighton.'

'Oh, Mr McLeod, I've been waiting ages for them to call for dinner. You did tell them it was served?'

'As per Miss St John's instructions I announced dinner at 7.30 p.m. sharp. However, it seems Lady Richenda has an engagement.'

This starchy pronouncement set Merry off once more. 'En-engagement,' she wailed, clutching her sides.'

'I fail to see the amusement,' said Rory, fixing me with his remarkable green eyes. Eyes that in the past had looked at me filled with laughter and with tenderness, now resembled the cool harshness of a perfect emerald. 'Can it be that Miss St John has taken it upon herself to announce a serious development in the fortunes of the family before being informed of said development by the head of the household?'

'Oh Rory,' said Merry, with the cheerful informality of a long standing servant, 'don't be so stuff...' She trailed off. The look he was giving her could have turned milk. 'I'm sorry, Mr McLeod,' she said and bobbed a small curtsy. Mrs Deighton looked from Rory to myself and sighed. 'Nothing is right in this house,' she said sadly.

'I must disagree,' said Rory, 'I believe that with the exception of the carrots all is in tolerable order. Merry, you will assist me at table tonight.

15

Change your apron.'

This I could not allow. 'Mr McLeod need I remind you it my duty along with yourself and first footman to oversee dinner.'

'I have orders that differ,' he said calmly, 'from the master.' He stressed the last word just enough to make me wince. 'Merry, hurry up and set an extra place. Mr Tipton will be joining us tonight.' He turned to me. 'I believe he will also be staying the night, so I require you to make ready a suitable bedroom, Miss St John.'

And with that, he turned and stalked out of the room. Mrs Deighton began to load the dumb waiter, muttering under her breath.

'Lord, Euphemia, what did you do to Rory to make him such a starched-up horror?' asked Merry.

I had thought to spare the feelings of both men by never mentioning their proposals to anyone else. My device had not been successful. I knew I should tell Merry off for addressing me so informally, but my heart wasn't it. Instead I gave a little shrug – a gesture my mother would have whipped me for using – and went to find little Daisy, another of our maids, to make ready the green bedroom.

The dinner party lasted long into the night. Rory, as butler, had the disputable joy of waiting up for the master to retire for the night. As I was awoken on more than one occasion during the night by shouts of excitement, it would seem the gentlemen had celebrated long into the night.

A new day dawned and I did not expect it to hold any surprises for me. Tipton had been Lord

Stapleford's right-hand man for some time now. His marrying Richenda did little more than formalise his position within the family. Of course, there would be the marriage day itself, but I had no doubt that it would be held in London amidst the grandest of the fashionable crowd. It might well be that Richenda (who I had never liked since she locked me in that cupboard) would be giving us all the gift of the family's absence for some time. I smiled at myself in my tiny mirror. I felt sure it was going to be a very good day.

Then someone screamed.

Chapter Two

In Which Things Become
Even More Disordered

As a servant I have come to hear many screams. The surprised squeak of a housemaid caught alone upstairs is a sharp piercing noise as opposed to, say, the wail of a scullery maid who has dropped a piece of fine china and is watching her next three months' wages lie shattered on the floor.

But this was a different kind of scream. This was the scream of a woman in fear of her life. I picked up my skirts and ran.

I had finally taken over the old housekeeper's room on the ground floor, so I rushed into the central hall with its large staircase. I hoped to be

17

able to ascertain the direction of the scream. Another scream broke over my ears echoing more loudly. The noise came from upstairs. Disregarding my duty to use the servants' stairs I pelted up the main staircase. Still the sound came from above. I rushed up the stairs once more and turned onto the wing with the main guests suites. As I did so, Rory darted out of one the servants' passageways onto the corridor.

'Where?' he gasped.

We both stopped and waited. Another scream gave us a direction. 'This way,' I cried.

'Euphemia!' shouted Rory. 'Wait!'

I flung open the door of Baggy Tipton's bedroom and almost fell over Daisy, our newest maid. She was lying on the floor soaking wet. Her eyes wide with terror as she turned her face to me. A large red stripe ran from her temple to her chin. In front of me stood Tipton his hand raised and in that hand a whip.

Without thinking I stepped over the sobbing maid and put myself between her and her assailant. Those treacherous eyes, the only part of him that had not been covered when he attacked Mrs Wilson, bored into mine. His hand was still raised. I lifted my chin and faced him as an equal daring him, without words, to do his worst.

I have no idea if he would have hit me, as Rory appeared that moment in the door way and let out a startled, 'Dear God in heaven! What has happened here?'

Tipton broke off from my gaze and looked past me to answer him. 'The shaving water was cold,' he said. He smoothed one hand through his hair as he dropped the whip onto a chair. 'Have some more sent up at once.' His voice chilled me. There was no note of anger nor regret. 'And have my lazy valet sent up to me,' he added. 'I need to be presentable this morning.'

Rory began to answer, stammering confirmation of his instructions. I helped Daisy to her feet. 'Come,' I said. 'We should go.'

I took her down the servants' stair because I did not wish her to be seen by the family. I was all too aware that they would be more likely to blame her than Tipton. 'I can't lose this job. I can't,' the poor girl kept whimpering.

'You won't,' I assured her. 'And very soon we will be rid of that man and Lady Richenda.'

'Oh no,' said Daisy. 'She said she'd make me her lady's maid.'

'If you follow her then you will be on the Tipton staff,' I pointed out gently.

We emerged into the warm light of the kitchen. Mrs Deighton came hurrying forward. 'Do you have any of your salve made up, Mrs Deighton?' I asked. 'Poor Daisy has had an accident.'

'Accident be blowed,' said our stalwart cook. 'The man's a menace.'

'Oh no,' said Daisy. 'He said the water was cold. It was my fault.'

'You shouldn't have been taking up shaving water to him in the first place,' I said.

'But he kept ringing and ringing.'

Rory entered the kitchen. He looked pale around the mouth. 'Where is that damn man's valet?'

'Avoiding his master is my best guess,' I said.

19

'I see,' said Rory. 'Then I think I will have a wee word with that mannie. Making a lassie do his dirty work. And you, Daisy, take the day off. Remain in your room and use compresses to ease the swelling. You cannot be seen with a face like that.' He gave me a challenging look.

He had no right to order about my staff, but I completely agreed with his decision. 'An excellent idea,' I said. 'If it wouldn't be too much trouble to get the scullery maid to take a portion of our meals up to Daisy, Mrs Deighton. I hate to cause you more work.'

'Think nothing of it,' said Mrs Deighton. 'I just have to burn those French kippers Mr Tipton is so fond of and then I will be right with you.'

'Haddock poached in milk for you, my girl. It'll set you up nice.'

And with that we all dispersed to our daily duties. I was careful to ensure that none of the maids were left alone with Tipton. He had never struck a member of our staff before, but I had no intention of giving him further opportunity.

The day went by with no pronouncement about the engagement. If Rory had not witnessed it too I would have begun to think it had been a fanciful dream. It was all very strange.

We had managed to get through luncheon with no further alarums. Sitting down to table had been only Tipton, Richenda and Lord Richard Stapleford, her brother. Her younger half-brother, Bertram, was away still overseeing the repairs to White Orchards, the estate he had impulsively bought and which was sliding slowly into the fens. For a brief time I had been housekeeper there

20

before the kitchen floor vanished in a pile of dust and we all came back home to roost, as it were.

Perhaps I thought they were waiting for Bertram to return before putting any plans into action, but he had never seemed of particular importance to his step brother and sister. Beside they knew, though none of us spoke of it, that he and I had worked against them.

I was desperately in need of Merry's companionship. Her jauntily outlook on life always shook me out of my gloom, but as best I could understand it, she had snuck away with our ex White Orchards footman and now chauffeur, Merrit, to show him 'some views.' I knew I should make a fuss when she returned, but between Rory and I we ran an extremely well-ordered house. And I, at least, was well aware of the strain of working for the Staplefords. Indeed they had only originally hired me, without references, because they simply could not keep staff.

The bell rang in the drawing room. It was time for Richenda to change her mind about dinner. This happened most days. I smoothed down my plain, black housekeeper's dress and made my way to the drawing room.

Opening the door I was surprised to see all three senior members of the household waiting for me. 'Wonderful news,' said Richenda, before I was even fully inside the room. 'We shall be having the wedding here.'

My jaw dropped.

'That won't be a problem, will it Euphemia?' she continued. 'I am thinking of only around three hundred guests.'

'Three hundred guests,' said Mrs Deighton, 'Three hundred! Lord above.' Mrs Deighton was sitting down in the kitchen for the first time in living memory.

'I suppose it is quite normal for a young woman to get married from her family home,' opined Rory.

'I thought they'd all head up to London,' I said. 'We can't accommodate that many people in the Hall and there is only one decent inn in the village.'

Rory shrugged. 'I expect people will motor down and back. It is all the rage now.'

'Hmm, trust Miss Richenda to try and do something fashionable,' said Mrs Deighton with vehemence. 'It will all end in tears, you see if it doesn't.'

'What we need to do,' I said, 'is get some realistic plans put together. We know she will reject most of the ideas, so we'll need to encourage her in the right direction.'

'Oh, Euphemia,' cried Mrs Deighton. 'I'm too old for all this. This is it! They'll send me packing without a pension!'

The cook threw her apron over her head and sobbed.

'Can we use caterers?' I asked Rory. 'Wouldn't that be fashionable?'

A loud wail came from beneath the apron.

'I think we may need something a wee bit more drastic than that.' said Rory. And for the first time in a very long time I saw his eyes begin to twinkle. 'And I think I know just the thing.'

22

Chapter Three

An Excess of Wildlife

'Aye, it's newts, sir. Baby ones.'

Lord Stapleford, Rory McLeod and I were standing in far too close proximity in Lord Stapleford's bathroom. Despite the tradition of shaving water being brought up boiling from the kitchen, Stapleford Hall was a comparatively new building and had a most advanced plumbing system.

We all stared down into the bathwater. It wriggled. 'Maid claimed they came out of the tap,' said Sir Richard in a bemused way. I struggled not to giggle. The situation was too ludicrous.

He turned on the cold tap again and clear water flowed. 'Must have been all the little blighters,' he said sounding relieved.

'We can hope so,' said the butler darkly.

'What do you mean, man?' demanded his master.

'It's just in my experience all infestation is not likely to be small.'

'Infestation? What the blithering...'

A loud scream curtailed the conversation. A shudder went down my spine, but almost at once I realised it was not Daisy.

'Me sister,' said Lord Stapleford and much to my surprise trotted as fast as a man in an overly tight suit could along the corridor. Rory did not follow, but leaned against the walk, his lip curling in a most unprofessional manner.

I cast him a suspicious look and ran after the figure of Lord Stapleford as it disappeared into his sister's boudoir. The sight that met my eyes would not have looked out of place on the vaudeville stage. Richenda stood on a chair, her skirts held high, screaming her head off. I noticed the thin legs of the chair shivered under her weight. 'My lady, I think you should come...'

'There! There!' shouted Richenda pointing at an overturned table. 'A monster!'

I bent down to examine the remnants of her mother's floral tea service that now lay in pieces across the floor. The pattern wasn't to my taste, but I couldn't see anything monstrous about it.

'The s-s-spout!' cried Richenda. The chair frame gave an alarming crack. Richard handed his sister swiftly down, and pushed her behind him. I advanced upon the tea set. The teapot was lying on its side towards her and away from me. Miraculously it remained intact. I turned it carefully towards me and a little greenish face peered back at me from the spout. I blinked in surprise and a small forearm pushed its way through the opening.

'Oh, the poor thing is stuck!' I said.

'Have you lost your mind?' screamed Richenda.

'Sure, it's only a full-grown newt, your ladyship,' said Rory, who had finally arrived. He took the teapot off me. 'I'll let the little fellow go in the garden.'

'What is a newt doing in my teapot?' demanded Richenda in a tone that would have impressed even my mother (who does imperious better than anyone else I have ever met.)

'It may be we have a wee infestation,' said Rory as Lord Stapleford made frantic hushing noises.

Richenda sagged against her brother, who let out an 'ooof' of surprise. 'Well, see there aren't any more of them, Euphemia,' she demanded.

However, as the day wore on the newts made more and more appearances. Mrs Deighton found them in the kettle. The scullery maid in her sink. Daisy found them in the vase water of the hall roses. There seemed to be no rhyme or rhythm to it. I could think of nothing except that all water to be consumed must be strained and then boiled. I had never heard of anyone dying from newt poisoning, but then I had never before come across an infestation.

This puzzled me greatly. I had grown up at a small vicarage in the country. If anywhere might have been expected to get wildlife in the water it was there. We certainly had our fair share behind the wainscoting, down in the cellars and even in the attics. My brother, little Joe, had a very fine collection of dried insect husks, small corpses and other matter that had once been animate that he delighted in leaving in the corner of the drawing room when the refined locals condescended to call on father. It had got him many a whipping. But the only time I remembered him bring newts into the house was when he had been playing down by the local river he was so fond of falling into.

At this thought I lifted my head and saw the boot boy, Sam, wander past my window whistling. A boot boy's lot is not a happy one. They work long hours for little reward. Sam is one of the better boot boys, who knows his life is best if he stays out of everyone's sight and does his job quickly and quietly. To see him drawing attention to himself by whistling in the garden was quite extraordinary.

It may seem strange that I am concentrating on the newts when a maid on my staff was recently attacked, but I am much saddened to say that the newts were by far the more unusual circumstance.

I closed the housekeeping accounts, pushed away from my desk and quickly made my way into the garden.

'Sam!'

The little boy's head came round so quickly I was afraid he'd do himself an injury. His eyes opened wide. I knew that look from old. 'My brother has just such a look on his face when he is caught out in mischief,' I said. 'Don't even think of running away from me, Sam.'

Slowly, as if being reeled in by a fishing line Sam made his way haltingly towards me. I noticed that his right hand was clenched deep in his pocket.

'What is in your hand?' I asked. 'No, Sam the other one.'

'Oh, that be'int anyfink I could show a lady like yourself, Miss St John.'

'Give,' I commanded.

The little fist hovered above my palm, quivered and then let fall two shillings.

'Good heavens, Sam! What have you been up

26

to?' I knew there was no way either the Staple-fords or Tipton would tip this, or indeed any amount, to have their shoes shined.

'I can't tell you, Miss.'

I took Sam firmly by the ear. 'You surely can and you surely will,' I said and with all the skill of an older sister I led him towards the kitchen. Rory appeared in the doorway. 'Ah, let the lad have his fun, Euphemia.'

'I require to know the nature of this fun, Mr Mc-Leod. I take it I need not remind you that as the senior male member of staff you are responsible for whatever misdemeanour this lad has under-taken.'

Rory reached over and undid my fingers from Sam's ears. 'Run along with you, lad. I'll sort this out.'

I looked up at him open mouthed in shock. My fingers tingled, not unpleasantly, from where he had touched them. I was furious. 'How dare you flout my authority, like that?'

'Me flout you? I thought you said the boy was my responsibility?'

'You know exactly what I mean,' I returned angrily.

'Sure you are gey bonnie when you're in a fash,' goaded Rory.

I took a deep breath. 'Did you pay that boy to put newts throughout the water system?'

'Once you've had an infestation, as I was just telling Lord Stapleford, you never know when you might get another. Makes the place most unsuitable for a grand function.'

'You idiot! He might well sell the Hall.'

27

'Rubbish! The three of 'em want this Hall mighty badly. It's their father's prize. Goodness knows why. I've suggested we have the plumbing system thoroughly cleaned and investigated. It needs a good going over if you ask me.'

'And I suppose they will find newts?' I said.

'Pockets here and there,' said Rory.

'But this just delays things. It doesn't solve matters.'

'A delay is all we need,' said Rory. 'Miss Richenda is determined to be wed on her birthday and that Hall plumbing certainly can't be refurbished by then.'

'You think you're very clever, don't you?'

Rory gave a self-satisfied shrug. 'All I know is I want the wedding off Mrs Deighton's shoulders and that wee weasel-faced shy–'

'Thank you, I get the idea. I have no more liking for Mr Tipton than you.'

Rory's face clouded. 'It's more than that,' he said. 'I tell you, Euphemia, there's something deeply wrong with that man.'

Chapter Four

The Bride Triumphs

'I'm beginning to wish I had never started this,' said Rory. His shoes and his trouser cuffs were unsuitably muddy. We were standing in the kitchen late at night when the family was abed.

28

Rory was holding two buckets full of newts.

I gave him a smile. 'You didn't think this through, did you?' I said. 'As soon as they think there is any chance the house will be fine, the wedding invites will be sent out.'

Rory sat down. 'We've been through some daft schemes, you and I, but this is the daftest yet.'

'Don't include me. This is entirely your plan. And to be honest I'm surprised at you. It seems outwith your normal character.'

Rory stirred one bucket with the end of Mrs Deighton's second best spoon. 'They would have got rid of her, you know,' he said. Probably without a pension too. I've seen it done before. She's got nae family, you know.'

'I'm afraid all you have done is delay the inevitable. Mrs Deighton is getting too old to run the kitchen of a large house.'

'Once Richenda and her husband have moved out...' began Rory.

'Who says they will? I hope it as much as you, but you know that ridiculous will for inheriting the Hall states that the children must stay in residence until they produce a legitimate heir, and whoever does so will inherit the Hall.'

'Aye, and don't tell me, it's about inheriting their father's blessing or some such nonsense rather than the Hall.'

'I am told that in London the name of Stapleford Hall, built by the Stapleford bankers, counts for something.'

'Aye right,' said Rory. 'But you're right it doesn't solve Mrs Deighton's problem.'

'We need to get her an undercook. I might have

been able to argue for that if the wedding had been here.'

'So you're saying it's all my fault?'

I leant over and touched Rory's hand briefly. 'You've risked your reputation and your position to protect an old lady from destitution. Your plan is ridiculous plan, but it is nobly ridiculous.'

'Och, well,' said Rory becoming alarmingly Scotch. 'I need away to tend to my newts.'

I retired to my chamber and began to wrack my brains for a solution. Goodness knew that the servants here had been the first to show kindness to me when I showed up at their door, dripping wet and then began to tug dead bodies around by the leg. It seemed so long ago. In two years I felt I had aged twenty. I certainly felt the weight of responsibility for my staff, but as I finally slipped into sleep I owned to myself that not only was I making no progress in bringing the Staplefords to justice, somehow along the way I had given up. I had lost myself in everyday activities. I lived my role as a housekeeper to the full and I was good at it. I was becoming a good servant. And a good servant would never bring Sir Richard down. Things had to change.

The next morning brought change in the departure of Mr Tipton. From the little smirks that Richenda kept giving herself in the mirror at breakfast I guessed something was afoot. However, although I had once been privy to many of this family's secrets they were doing a very good job now of keeping me out.

'I shall be writing a letter this morning,' announced Richenda. 'It is a most important one and I do not care to be disturbed by the maids. See to it that the fire is lit in the little morning room and the room well-aired by the time I have finished breakfast.'

If Richenda had been a tea-and-toast-breakfast type of lady this might have been a problem, but even as I hurried away to arrange matters she was tucking into her second kipper.

Later, I was clearing the breakfast things when Bertram Stapleford, the twins' younger brother, burst into the room. 'It's not all gone, is it Euphemia? I could eat an elephant!'

'I think we may have a small amount of elephant steak left, sir,' I said with a smile. Bertram had been away for the house for several months.

'It's good to see you again, Euphemia – I mean Miss St John,' said Bertram.

If I was surprised at his sudden willingness to speak to me again it was not an unwelcome surprise and I immediately busied myself with bringing him breakfast things, as I had once done at White Orchards.

He looked up at me as I set the place before him. 'Just like old times,' he said ruefully. 'I took a look at the house on the way here.'

'And how fares it?'

He sighed. 'They have had to take the roof off now.'

'Oh no!' I cried.

'Rotten joists or some such thing.'

'But it is only just built!'

'I think "thrown together" would be a more accurate description than built. Still, you will have me back among your number for some time until

31

all the repairs are put in order. There is no chance of my even selling the house now its true state has been revealed.'

'I am sorry, sir.'

'Are you?' asked Bertram, a strange look in his dark eyes. 'At least I shall be around to see all this wedding malarkey at first hand.'

'Is that of interest to you, sir?'

'Richenda insisting she marries on her birthday, the same day she comes into her full inheritance? And considering who she is marrying? I'm far from clear if my brother has played a blinder or if my stepsister is finally about to trump him.'

'You mustn't talk to me about the family like that!' I exclaimed.

'Come on, Euphemia! You know as well as I do machinations are afoot. And I for one would rather be on hand to see them through and to offer you...'

I gave him a strongly repressing look.

'Oh yes, very well. Pass the marmalade please.'

I puzzled over Mr Bertram's remarks, but could make no real sense of them. The business of the house continued as usual. Richenda went up to London to ready her trousseau. Sir Richard gave her a lavish spending allowance and she came back with two motor cars full of boxes. She floated around the place, very much the bride-to-be in all her glory, even though no venue had been set nor invites issued. I decided to merely be content that Tipton stayed away and to avoid thinking about the helter-skelter of planning that would ensue once a place had been determined.

When Richenda returned from London, her

mood changed. She took every opportunity to goad me and I took every opportunity to remain calm and professional. I had learnt that nothing infuriated her more than someone not rising to her attacks.

Tipton had still not returned and she was behaving less and less like a bride-in-waiting. I couldn't help wondering if it were all going to amount to nothing after all. The other sign that things were different was the inordinate amount of letters she was writing.

Then one morning Richenda erupted into my parlour. As the senior female servant I now had a small sitting room where I could study the house accounts. I had managed to rid it of most of the monstrous old, dark furniture my predecessor had favoured, and I had also been ruthless with the remnants of Victoriana. The result was a light, airy space with minimal furnishing, but a sense of harmony. My one luxury was the vase of fresh flowers I kept on the central table. The bright colours of nature always cheered me and reminded me that there was a world beyond the control of the Staplefords; the natural world where no matter how they wished their laws did not hold sway.

It was a good space, but an ecstatic Richenda overwhelmed it. She waved a letter far too close to my face and announced, 'She is coming!'

'Queen Mary?' I asked without thinking.

Richenda's face clouded. 'No, Euphemia, I am referring to my chief bridesmaid.'

She thrust the letter further under my nose and I managed to read the name of a minor member of a European Royal House.

'Er, congratulations.'

'She is a relation on my late mother's side,' Richenda was now pacing the room in earnest. 'We must of course ensure no one knows. For her safety.'

'Of course,' I said, thinking that telling your housekeeper wasn't exactly the best way to begin a campaign of silence.

Richenda stopped and looked at me with her head on one side. 'Though these things do tend to get out.'

'I won't say a word.'

Richenda's face became mulish. 'Imagine if anyone knew,' she said slowly and carefully, 'every society photographer... Such a shame about Lady Grey. I wonder if Bertram knows her replacement?'

I gasped. 'You're not going to ask him, are you?'

Richenda blinked and noticed I was still there. 'Tactless, you think? He'd never have married her. She smelled too much of shop even for our liberal-leaning Bertram.'

I swallowed. 'I really have no notion of Mr Bertram's love life, but I am aware he thought highly of...'

'I wasn't asking for your opinion.'

'Of course not. But what it is exactly you wish my help with?'

'Nothing,' snapped Richenda. She slammed the door on her way causing my little vase to rock wildly.

I stared after her a strange thought crossing my mind. Could it be the Richenda had no one else to tell about her bridesmaid coup? We had the occasional party at Stapleford Hall, but without exception the guests were connected to Lord Stapleford's constituency business or the family's actual business interests. I closed my accounts books. When I had arrived at the household, Richenda had been returning to the house after a period of exile imposed by her father. Her interests in the suffragettes' movement, and the fact that she had set up a house for fallen women, had not impressed her father. Richenda was unconditionally loyal to her brother, who she failed to see was made in the same mould as her father. I remain unsure if Richenda does support causes that I too would like to champion or was simply set on annoying her father. Whichever it was it had left her without high society friends of her own to the extent her housekeeper was the best person she had to boast of her royal connections. All those letters she had been writing must have been her search for a bridesmaid. I shook my head, pushing away these welcome thoughts. If I continued on the vein I would begin feeling sorry for Richenda and I could not allow such a weakness while Sir Richard Stapleford and Tipton were still weaving their various machinations. Of course, it didn't help that I had no idea what those machinations might be. Running Stapleford Hall at full strength took a lot of time and attention. We might have been within motoring distance of London, but it could just as well have been a world away as far as news of real events was concerned.

Since accepting this appointment, I had found

35

out far more than was necessary about the linen count of Stapleford Hall, and how many greens the family was likely to consume during the summer season. I knew their intimate details, but I knew nothing about their activities. Sir Richard had sewn me up tightly in a web of domesticity. I was too busy to be bored, but I was also totally ineffective in challenging the Stapleford misdemeanours. I had painted myself into a corner.

I had had some hope that the wedding would allow me access to more information, but Rory's newt scheme, albeit a philanthropic idea, had changed all that. At least Mrs Deighton was safe for now.

I, on the other hand, was stuck in the doldrums.

Chapter Five

Announcements of Varying Levels of Concern

The day began brightly, beautifully and with the whole household running like clockwork. Only Richenda and Bertram remained in residence. Bertram had declared to Rory the day was so fine he was going to walk the land and see if he could put up some pigeons. I served Richenda a solitary (but hearty) breakfast and observed her to be in an unusually quiet mood.

Then at eleven o'clock a delivery of the trousseau came in on the train, accompanied by Lady Stapleford. Lord Stapleford's widow was very French. She had been living in Brighton, and she disliked me intently. My first sight of her was of a figure draped in black lace topped by a large and remarkably ugly hat. She was dabbing an overlarge handkerchief to her eyes. As I made my way across the hallway to welcome her she exclaimed, 'To think it has all come to this!'

I believe that even my mother, with her vast knowledge of etiquette and the right things to say, might have been somewhat flummoxed at this opening. I folded my hands neatly as I approached and bobbed a small curtsey. 'Lady Stapleford, it is an honour to welcome you back to Stapleford Hall. I am afraid it will take a few minutes to air your rooms, as I was not aware of your arrival today. If you would perhaps like to take tea in the morning room I could ensure everything is perfect for your arrival.'

'I am not a guest,' snapped Lady Stapleford, lowering her handkerchief and snapping it violently towards me. 'This is my home.'

And there it was; the heart of the matter. Even I did not know who technically owned Stapleford Hall at this time. Richard Stapleford paid my wages and he was the eldest son of the late Sir Richard Stapleford, so it was to him I deferred, but I had no idea how Lady Stapleford fitted into all this. Certainly no one had seen fit to build her a dower house. A closer scrutiny of her clothing suggested that bows and turns had been made over. I was not up with the latest fashions. Richenda never bothered to dress well in the country, but I knew all too well the signs of made over clothing. Hadn't Mother and I done it for years? I was beginning to feel sorry for Lady Stapleford, when her voice cut razor like through my thoughts.

'And what have you done with my son?'

She meant, of course, Bertram. She had been Lord Stapleford's second wife. 'I believe he is out rough shooting,' I said.

'That is not what I meant,' sneered the lady. 'I was asking about your activities with my only boy.'

It took a moment or several for the coarseness of the question to find its way through the fog of my brain. When it did so, I confess, I suddenly embodied an outstanding impression of a goldfish. I simply did not have the words.

My rescue came from an unexpected source. ''Ere yous, watch what yer doing with 'em cases. The buckle on that's worth more than you get in a year, you clodhopping dunderbrain.'

A pertly pretty young woman, dressed in the dark clothes of a servant, but with a far too dashing hat tipped to one side, swept in. 'Lord, these country bumpkins. Beggin' pardon your ladyship, but there's not a gnat's worth of brain between the lot of them.' She was carrying a small case.

Lady Stapleford's direct gaze didn't break from mine. 'Indeed, Suzette, you will find matters in the country can be quite parochial, even basic.'

'Don't know about that ma'am. But that footman didn't look like he'd ever seen a proper lady's luggage before. I kept the jewel case meself, not knowing you I was to trust like.' She turned her attention to me. 'And who's this? The village idiot?'

'This,' said Lady Stapleford, 'is Lord Stapleford's housekeeper, Euphemia St John. She was previously my son's housekeeper at that terrible estate. She affects a great fondness for the men of my family.'

'Oh, like that, is it?' said Suzette. 'Then I think it's right condescending for you to come 'ere at all. Nothing's unpacked. I could have us out of here in a trice, my lady. I'm not sure it is cognisant with your ladyship's dignity to remain.' The expression on her face was insolence itself, but I noted a certain eagerness when she talked about departing. This new lady's maid of Lady Stapleford's had some secrets of her own, I decided.

'Lady Stapleford,' I began calmly, 'I am aware that you have been living in a retired manner since your widowhood, but I can assure you any rumours that might have reached your ears referencing any misdemeanours of your son would refer solely to his impulsive purchase of White Orchards which has been a sad trial to him.'

'Oh la-di-da,' trilled Suzette. 'Talks like a regular book, she does.'

'Suzette, oversee that footman taking my cases to my rooms. He will be using the servants' stair. You remember my explaining the house layout?'

Suzette bobbed a small curtsey. 'At once ma'am,' she said and then to my utter astonishment behind her mistress's back she thumbed her nose at me.

'My lady, I am the new butler, Rory McLeod. Can I be of service?'

I spun round to see Rory had appeared. Over

39

these past months I had noticed he taken the butler prerequisite of appearing silently very much to heart.

'Ah, yes, the Scotchman,' said Lady Stapleford somewhat enigmatically. She swept past us both and mounted the stairs. 'My maid will inform you of my requirements.'

We turned and watched her in respectful silence as she disappeared over the first landing.

'Would that maid be the cheeky wee miss I just passed on the servants' stair?' asked Rory.

'She thumbed her nose at me,' I said.

'I was thinking you were looking a wee bit pale. I gather you've no idea how to deal with such rudeness?'

'Even the boot boy wouldn't think to do that to me.' I said. 'At least not to my face,' I added on reflection.

'Well, she'll get short shift from me if she tries that.'

I sighed. 'She won't. You're a man.'

'I'm aware of that,' said Rory, 'but I fail to see why that should make a difference.'

'I know,' I said. 'It's a female thing. I'd better go and inform Lady Richenda her stepmother is here.'

'Send Merry,' advised Rory. 'You need to work on your authority.'

I found Merry in the kitchen. 'Ooh, this will set the cat among the pigeons,' she said gleefully. 'Do you think she's come back to oversee the wedding?'

'She's more likely to be back because she's out of funds,' said the cook.

'Mrs Deighton,' I said shocked. 'It's not like you to gossip.'

'I knows Lady Stapleford. Me and her go way back. Can't say we were ever on friendly terms – and if she took a dislike, like she sometimes did, she could make life hard for you, but she and I, we rubbed along alright. She liked my French chicken. Said it reminded her of the old days.'

'Well, she has always disliked me,' I said.

'Your arrival did sort of start the downfall of the Staplefords, didn't it?' said Merry.

'It was hardly my fault.'

'No,' said Mrs Deighton, 'things were set to implode for some time before Euphemia arrived.'

'What do you mean?' I asked suddenly side-tracked. Mrs Deighton never talked about the days before my arrival and I had forgotten how well she knew the family.

'Like you said,' she answered annoyingly, 'I'm not one to gossip.'

'Right Merry, go and tell Richenda now before her stepmother introduces herself and then get Daisy to make up a bed for her lady's maid. If I'm any judge of character we won't be seeing her downstairs for her dinner with us. It will be a tray in her room.'

'That's how it should be,' said Mrs Deighton. 'Like you should eat in your parlour, Euphemia, and not with us.'

I felt a tears start to my eyes. 'Mrs Deighton!'

'Now, now, my dear. I'm not saying that's what I would like, but if we're going to be descended on by a load of toffs we should get ourselves sorted.'

I felt someone close behind me, so close I could feel the heat of them. 'I do not think,' said Rory's voice, 'that the matter of which servant attends the communal dining is a matter for the cook. It is a matter for Miss St John and myself to discuss.'

'Well, I don't know, I'm sure,' said Mrs Deighton.

'I do,' said Rory firmly. 'I am also informing you that tonight's dinner will need extra courses. It is no longer a simple affair. I have been informed over the telephone machine that both Sir Richard Stapleford and Mr Tipton will be present tonight. This means that all the senior members of the family will be together for the first time since the late Sir Richard Stapleford's demise. I trust you will be able to create a suitable repast?'

Mrs Deighton gave him a look of horror and then disappeared into the scullery calling for her maid. Rory took me by the elbow and steered me out the kitchen. 'I need a word,' he said. His breath was hot and close to my ear. I am ashamed to say it didn't feel unpleasant. In fact a strange tingle ran down my spine. My lacings must be too tight.

However, I didn't have time to respond as the garden door flew open and a flushed, but happy-looking Bertram entered the room. He had a broken shotgun over his shoulder and several pigeons strung together. 'Look at these, Euphemia,' he cried. 'Look at these. 'I've not lost my eye.'

'I think you may find that Mrs Deighton will be delighted to have those,' said Rory. 'We will be a very full house tonight.'

42

'Your mother has arrived,' I said, 'and your brother and Mr Tipton are expected later.'

The bright enthusiasm in Bertram's face faded. 'Oh Lord,' he said. 'It'll be nothing but wedding plans.'

'I fear so, sir,' said Rory. The two men exchanged a look of understanding from which I was excluded. Bertram then stomped off to the kitchen leaving a trail of muddy footprints.

'The floor,' I cried.

'Leave it,' said Rory. 'I need to talk to you.'

'But!'

'No one's going to see it back here,' he said and then, there is no other word for it, shoved, yes shoved, me into my own parlour.

'Good heavens!' I said as he shut the door smartly behind us, 'what has got into you, Rory McLeod?'

For an answer, the butler took me roughly in his arms and kissed me.

Chapter Six

In Which Matters Progress

I have been brought up not to think about kissing much less to indulge in it, but I own the sensation was not unpleasant. Rory had soft, warm lips and his arms around me felt reassuringly strong. For a moment I did surrender to his embrace and I confess I enjoyed it. But then with ringing clarity

I heard my mother's voice in my head, 'The son of a grocer. The son of a grocer with an Earl's granddaughter.'

Rory let me go. I stepped away from him to help us both resist further temptation. He was breathing heavily and there was a look in his eyes I did not recognise. A glance in the mirror over the mantle showed me my dishevelled hair, a pink blush across my cheeks and a certain wild look in my own eyes.

Rory took a step forward. I took another step back. 'Enough,' I said, holding up my hand. Even to my own ears my voice sounded less than forbidding.

'Och lass, I cannae keep up this charade any longer. We were made for each other, and you know it.'

As I looked into his glorious green eyes, my heart beat faster and my breath came quicker. My voice answered him seemingly without my volition. 'Yes,' I said. 'We are.'

It was encouragement enough and before I had time to take another breath I was in his arms once more. This time I made no pretence at resistance. We might be miles apart on the social scale accordingly to my mother, but right here, right now I was a housekeeper and he was the butler. We were social equals and any secret history I might have could remain secret for the rest of my life as far as I was concerned. In Rory's arms I felt I had come home. I felt safe and secure, and loved and cherished, and other stronger emotions that do not need to be named in words. For all I cared the rest of the world could go to blazes.

This time it was Rory who broke away. 'Wait,' he said. 'I will do this right. I want you for my wife, Euphemia. This is the last time I will propose to you. Will you have me?'

'Yes,' I said and I meant it.

What would have happened next I do not know, but the front door bell rang.

'Stapleford and Tipton.' Rory uttered their names as if they were the worst swear words he knew. He caught my hands and held them tightly. 'You said yes,' he said. 'Remember that.'

I smiled up at him. 'I meant it.'

Rory stopped with the door half open. 'Leave it to me to tell them? We'll need to pick our moment.'

I nodded. 'I can't afford to lose this position – my family.'

'I know, love. I'll make it right.' He winced. 'We may have to wait until after Richenda's wedding.'

I sighed. 'I think that is beyond doubt.'

The doorbell rang again. Rory nodded and closed the door behind him. I realised this would doubtless be the first time the door of Stapleford Hall had been answered on the second ring. I was deeply glad it was my fault.

I made my way towards the kitchen to see how Mrs Deighton was coping. 'My stepmother!' bellowed Lord Stapleford from the hallway. I heard the quiet murmur of Rory's reply. 'Looks like you'll have to run the gauntlet, Baggy.'

'I think we can drop the nickname now, don't you?' said Tipton in a stronger tone than I ever remember him using. 'Your sister doesn't like it.'

'What rot! Let's go meet the mater.'

45

'I have met her before.' The voices were crossing the hall now.

'Yes, but not as a prospective member of the family.'

'I don't think there's anything prospective about now, old boy,' said Tipton. 'Once I had the venue sorted I put in straight in *The Times*. Should be in the evening edition.'

'Blast it, man. You haven't even told me.'

'I can assure,' said Tipton sounding exceedingly smug, 'you'll be pleased.'

'Not gone and rented Westminster Abbey or some such place, have you?' said Sir Richard. I could hear he sounded nervous. It occurred to me he felt obligated to foot the bill. I entered the kitchen with a spring in my step. 'How goes it, Mrs Deighton?'

Our cook looked up from the big range, which was covered in pots and pans. Her face ruddy and slick with sweat, she nodded grimly. 'They'll be having a fine meal tonight. One of them posh London hotels couldn't do better. But Lord knows I'll have to get Daisy off to the market first thing tomorrow or there won't be in a thing in the house to eat tomorrow night. I'm even using Mr Bertram's pigeons. He always was a good shot. Not a lot of lead in them.'

'Doesn't that mean he almost missed,' I said, but I had already lost the cook's attention.

Merry reported that she'd had the gentlemen's rooms in order for a couple of days and would prefer, if I had no objection, to do the turndowns and last-minute niceties while they were at dinner. 'I know one of 'em about to be married

46

'n' all,' she said bluntly, 'but it's never stopped no toff to my knowledge trying to feel up a maid.'

'Quite,' I said repressively. 'I'm sure you know how to attend to the gentlemen discreetly and invisibly.'

'If I do get spotted I just lift up my skirts and leg it,' said Merry. 'You'd better to the same too, Daisy.'

Daisy's face had healed well. She was lucky. However, she had developed a habit of starting at any loud noise. 'I think we'll take Daisy off the upstairs work,' I said. 'If you don't mind, Daisy, I think I'll assign you to the kitchen for a while. Mrs Deighton is going to need a lot of help with supplies and readying meals. We really have more than enough maids to deal with the extra work upstairs, but down here it's going to be tight.' A worried frown formed on the girl's face. 'Don't worry,' I said, 'you'll still be paid as a maid and you will return to those duties in future once we know what the house requirements will be after the wedding.'

'You mean the staff will be changing?' asked Mrs Deighton.

'I really have no idea,' I said. 'When I hear whether the Tiptons will be making their home here, or taking staff elsewhere, I will tell you.'

'I suppose I'll be expected to act as lady's maid,' said Merry grouchily.

'I think not,' I said. 'Lady Stapleford has brought a maid with her, Suzette. I wouldn't be surprised if she also tended to Richenda.'

'Oh that's good,' said Merry in a tone that clearly indicated it wasn't and flounced off. Merry might dislike being at Richenda's beck and call, but there had often been gifts of old scarves, hats, gloves and on occasion even money as extra perks. Richenda might sway with her moods, but with Merry she could be exceedingly generous.

However, later in the evening, Richenda did call on Merry's services. I couldn't help but wonder if she had taken to Suzette about as well as I had. Time also showed I had been right in believing the maid would send down for food rather than join us. Mrs Deighton huffed about it, but she was a creature of habit and much preferred the normal evening arrangements.

We always ate before the family and this night our meal was more rushed than normal. Rory and I sat opposite each other, stealing glances and smiles when we hoped the others weren't watching.

Of course, we served dinner together. Every time we brushed past each other or our fingers touched in the passing of a dish I felt electric tingles run up and down my spine. I knew such feelings belonged between the pages of a bad gothic romance, such as I had had to hide under the bed from my mother when I was younger, but I didn't care. Mr Bertram broke in on my thoughts. 'Euphemia is there anything wrong? You don't seem yourself.'

'Bertram, honestly, don't address the servants during dinner unless you need more peas,' said Lady Stapleford.

Bertram didn't answer his mother, but I felt his eyes following me for the rest of the meal. I tried desperately to think solely of the fish sauce and keep my blushes in check.

The meal seemed interminable, but finally Tipton stood up and called for champagne as he had an announcement to make.

'Finally,' said Sir Richard. 'I take you are going to tell us where you have arranged the wedding and not make some maudlin speech about your bride-to-be. Because if you are, you can damn well make do with claret.'

'Richard,' said Lady Stapleford sternly, 'why is the wedding not being held here?'

'Because Richenda wants to invite more people than we can decently house,' said Sir Richard. 'Wants a great show by all accounts.'

'I am in the room,' said his sister dangerously.

Rory slid silently into place with the ice buckets. Sir Richard gave a careless one handed gesture and Rory opened the bottles and began to disrupt the drink.

Tipton stood up. 'I am proud and happy to announce that after discussing matters with my extended family we have decided the best way to welcome my bride is hold the wedding at The Court!'

There were gasps from around the table. 'You mean your grand-uncle, the Earl, has agreed to host Richenda's wedding?' asked Lady Stapleford in a faint voice.

'Yes,' said Tipton, 'and, my dear, you can have as many damned wedding guests as you please.'

'Oh Tippy,' cried Richenda, launching up to throw her arms around her betrothed's neck and incidentally spilling blackcurrant sauce all over the fine white linen tablecloth, 'Oh Tippy!'

'For Heaven's sake, Richenda, think of your

49

poor father's memory and have some decorum,' snapped Lady Stapleford. 'It is very kind of Tipton's great-uncle to offer, but...'

'I am having my wedding at The Court!' said Richenda, 'and nothing you can do will stop me. We are not even blood.'

Lady Stapleford stood up. 'Am I to be so insulted in my house?" she asked looking directly at Bertram.

'I'm afraid I took the liberty of sending the notice to *The Times*,' said Tipton. 'It would look very awkward if we cried off now.'

'But we have not even decided the date,' said Lady Stapleford.

'My birthday,' said Richenda.

'I can see when I am not needed,' said Lady Stapleford.

'Stepmother,' appealed Sir Richard, 'my twin is overexcited. I expect she never thought it would happen. Her getting married.'

'Richard,' cried Richenda. 'How dare you. I'll have you know I've had more than one offer. I was waiting for the right man.' She gave Tipton a look so sickening I feared it would clot the custard. 'Besides I have news of my own. As you all know I went to a most excellent finishing school and while I was there I was invited on a weekend away, where I met a certain personage.'

'Is this going to be a long story, Richenda,' said Bertram, casting a nervous look at his still upright mother, 'only I don't think now is quite the time.'

'A certain personage of a Royal Household,' continued Richenda in a loud voice. 'Her Royal

Highness – (I apologise to my readers, but for reasons that will become clear I cannot in good faith name the person in question) – and she has agreed to be my chief bridesmaid.

'Good heavens,' said Lady Stapleford, and collapsed down in her seat. 'Who did you say, Richenda?'

Richenda repeated the name. Tipton clapped. 'Oh jolly good, old girl,' he cried. 'This will set the mater and my great-aunt up. They were a little concerned... But never mind that now. Where's your telephone thingy, I must let them know.'

'If you will follow me, Mr Tipton,' I said and led him from the room. I ached to return to the dining room and watch the fallout from this discussion, but now the champagne had been served it was up to the footman to clear the dishes when the ladies withdrew. My duty lay with making sure the tea was laid waiting for them and that there was more cake. Richenda always wanted more cake.

Chapter Seven

In Which Things Start to Unravel

I observed from within one of the copious hidden passageways the entrance into the drawing-room. Observed is perhaps a little overstating the matter. The passageway led directly to the kitchen, opening with a false section of wall into the drawing-room. I had the opening perhaps a quarter of an inch ajar and my eye pressed to the opening. It was highly unprofessional, but I wanted to see how things unfolded.

I could see Lady Stapleford's elbow moving over the tea-tray. 'My dear Richenda, as you sadly have no mother alive, I feel I must do my duty by you as your poor father would have wished,' was her opening salvo.

'That is so kind of you, Stepmama,' answered Richenda. 'After all I know well you always advocated for me when father and I were estranged.' I could imagine the bitter smile on her face. Lady Stapleford had wanted nothing to do with Lord Stapleford's twins. They were a reminder there was a wife before her and more painfully that her beloved, Bertram, was not the elder son of the house as she undoubtedly felt he should be. Though, to be fair, Bertram had never showed any such ambition, preferring to shun the family business and manage his own affairs. Thinking about Bertram was unaccountably making me uncomfortable, so I pushed all thoughts of him aside and peered closer.

'Richenda, I am aware your father sent you to an excellent finishing academy, but you have not, I believe, kept up with fashionable society. I think you said your chief bridesmaid wasn't actually a pupil at the academy. How close has your communication been?'

'We have exchanged letters from time to time. Her Highness has an interest in rescuing fallen women in her own country.'

'How laudable,' said Lady Stapleford making it

quite clear she meant exactly the opposite. 'But she hasn't visited you recently? She certainly didn't visit the Hall when I was in residence. In your own mother's time?'

Richenda made a non-committal and unlady-like grunt.

'And the company she met you in, was un-exceptional?'

'Father arranged for me to stay with the cousin of a girl at the school.'

'So not even a fellow pupil. I see.'

'You see what, Stepmama? Enlighten me.'

If I had been Lady Stapleford I would have stepped outside teapot-throwing range at the tone in Richenda's voice.

'I mean, Richenda, that you are, to phrase it in vulgar parlance, marrying up. Tipton might be – well – might be what he is, but he is directly con-nected to an earldom. You, my dear are the daughter of a hereditary peerage that is only in its second generation. You may have money, but you smell of trade.'

'How ... how dare you?'

'Easily, my dear. As my whole family was aware I married down.'

'For money,' said Richenda. Her voice was tight.

'Indeed,' replied Lady Stapleford, 'as your Tippy is doing. I own it quite freely. I prefer luxury to elite poverty.'

'Other than insulting me, Stepmama, is there a point you are attempting to make?'

'It is merely this, my dear. Once your "friend" has checked your connections, or rather once her family have, I think it very unlikely she will consent to come to your wedding at all. No matter whose home you might borrow.'

'Rubbish,' snapped Richenda. 'You don't know her.'

'And neither do you. You have some fleeting acquaintance based on dabbling in charity for some romantic high ideals, but the real world is about practicalities and position. I tell you she will not be allowed to attend.'

There was a short pause. 'I do not believe you to be right,' said Richenda, but I could hear the doubt in her voice.

'Then we will say no more about it,' said Lady Stapleford. 'Time will tell which of us is right.' She nibbled the edge of a cake, swallowed, and then said, sugar dripping from her voice, 'Such a pity you told Tipton before me. I could have predicted he would head straight off and tell his family. Anything to shore up your reputation. Such a gentlemanly thought. Quite unlike him.'

I edged further back into the passageway and let the door close completely. The conversation had become too uncomfortable for even my curiosity. I headed back into the kitchen which was awash with dirty dishes and people scurrying about. There was no sign of Rory or any of the upstairs maids. I decided I had wasted enough time and went to check that everything upstairs was in readiness. I hoped to avoid Suzette. I had yet to think of a stratagem to deal with her blunt rudeness.

The maids had done their work well. There was nothing for me to correct. I was about to depart down the servants' stair when a door opened. "Ere, you up here to take me tray?' Suzette stood in the doorway of her mistress's room, her hands on her hips.

'No,' I said calmly. 'It would not be usual for a housekeeper to wait on any servant in this or any house.'

'So 'ho the bleeding 'eck is going to take it away 'cos I don't think my lady would like the smell of this greasy fish sauce stinking up her room.'

'If you choose to take your meals away from the rest of the staff, then it would be expected you would do so in your own room.'

'You mean that pokey little attic cupboard, you've given me?'

'If you are unhappy with your accommodation then we can look at things in the morning. I am afraid it will not be possible to move you tonight. And I imagine no one has come to take your tray as no one would have imagined you would have thought it fit to eat in your mistress's rooms.'

Suzette gave a loud sniff. 'Well, seeing as you're here, you can take it.'

'No,' I said, 'it is not my place. You may speak to Daisy about the delivery of your meals.'

'Not your place,' sneered Suzette. 'I've 'eard a lot about your place. Your position. You ain't no different from me.'

'To be sure, we are all God's creatures,' I said and made my escape down the staircase. A ringing "Ere, you!' followed me, but I chose to ignore it.

Back on the ground floor I made my way to the butler's pantry. Rory was counting out the silver that had been used at dinner. He looked up at my entrance and his whole face came alight. 'Sure, you're a bonnie sight.'

I closed the door behind me. 'We must be careful,' I said. 'I don't think things are going well upstairs.'

Rory stood and took my hands in his. 'Sure, why would they not be. They've a wedding to celebrate. A grand house to hold it in and a bride and groom, who seems pleased to be together.'

It was on the tip of my tongue to tell Rory all I had overheard, but as I looked into his luminous green eyes and saw the affection there, I could only think of how they would cloud over if he knew I had been interesting myself in the affairs of my betters. Each to their own world was very much Rory McLeod's rule. So I smiled and said, 'I don't know. I think people always get a bit edgy before weddings, so many things to organise.'

He drew me closer, let go of my hands and wrapped his arms around me. I found his shoulder was at the exact right height to rest upon, 'Well, I can tell you, lass, there will be no troubles before our wedding. My family will adore you. And I must meet your mother. I suppose I should also be asking your little brother's permission to marry you,' he said with a laugh. 'Do you think that would get him on my side or would a quarter of jellybeans be a better way into his good books?'

I felt as if a bucket of cold water had been poured over me. For all his mischievousness, Little Joe was the apple of my mother's eye and had imbibed all of her ideas about class. He thought my pretending to me a maid was a grand, roman-

56

tic adventure, but he would not understand my decision to marry out of my class.

'Euphemia? Is there something wrong? Do you not want me to meet your family? Am I not good enough?'

I put my hand up to touch his face. 'Not good enough? You are the best man I have ever met. Anyone should be proud to welcome you into their family.' Should be. I did believe that, but I also knew that they would not be. Perhaps Lady Stapleford and I had more in common than I might wish.

'Then what's wrong?'

'Suzette,' I said, 'Lady Stapleford's maid. She is openly rude and clearly does not respect my authority.'

'Well, all ladies' maids tend to be a bit hoity-toity.'

'No, she's not that. Not at all. She thumbed her nose at me in the Hall behind Lady Stapleford's back.'

'Thumbed her nose at you,' said Rory and laughed. 'You'll have to put a stop to that right quick. I take it she has a little too much of the common for a lady's maid?'

'Oh, she's common, alright,' I said.

'Och, Euphemia, if she speaks common then that will be it. She'll be embarrassed. It's not everyone that can move in society, like you do, without being made to feel inferior. You know half the time I have to remind myself you're not a toff the way you speak and act. I'll be gey proud to have you seen on my arm.' He kissed my forehead. 'Trust me. That will be it. Suzette's being defensive about being out of her class. Can't say I blame her. This world of the Staplefords wouldn't do for me. I'm a grocer's son and proud of it. What did your father do?'

'He was a vicar,' I said.

'Oh, so I'll be the one marrying up,' said Rory, giving me another squeeze.

Oh Rory, if only you knew, I thought, but I could not bring myself to explain. He was so happy. We were so happy. I didn't want to destroy this moment I told myself. I'll explain later. Before we marry, of course, but there will be time to sort all that out later. But I really had no idea of how I was going to sort any of it out. What was it Lady Stapleford had said about romance, and it not fitting well with practicalities and position? Well, I was going to have to make them fit.

Chapter Eight

In Which Breakfast Becomes Too Eventful

The next day dawned bright and sunny. Daisy set off before breakfast to visit the local markets and place orders with our suppliers. The blackcurrant stain had come out overnight after being soaked in Mrs Deighton's secret recipe for stain removal. Lady Stapleford had sent word she would breakfast at noon in her bedchamber, so breakfast could be the normal informal affair Sir Richard preferred and which Mrs Deighton could create with her eyes closed.

Tipton had left straight after breakfast to further the wedding plans and Richenda was closeted with fashion plates, considering whether or not to upgrade her wedding outfit.

Rory was humming softly to himself and going about the place with his head held high. Probably even the robin in the garden had caught a good, few juicy worms this morning. All in all, the day was showing signs of being excellent for all but me. My night's sleep had been disturbed my dreams of my mother's furious tirade when I told her of my marriage and of Mr Bertram wandering lost and disconsolate through endless rooms seeking something he had lost, and try as I might, I could not help him. Merrit came in from the garden, whistling and hold a basket of various fruits and vegetables. 'These help, Mrs D? Get you through lunch?'

'Oh, you're a marvel, young man,' said Mrs Deighton planting a smacking kiss on his cheek. Really, everyone was revoltingly happy with themselves and each other.

I needed to be away from the lot of them, so I decided to inspect the flowers in the hallway. Merry did these and she always did them faultlessly, but with the extra work we all had on, I decided to double check. I had triumphantly found my first dead-head when the telephone clanged. It was just as well I wasn't holding the vase as I still cannot get used to the wretched machine's sharp interruptions. I did not even consider answering it. This was Rory's domain. He arrived quickly, moving smoothly, but never breaking into what one might call a trot or a run. He was definitely getting the business of being a butler well in hand.

'Lord Stapleford's residence. Stapleford Hall.' (Pause.) 'Miss Richenda does not currently have a secretary. Would you like me to fetch her ladyship?' (Pause.) 'I see.' (Pause.) 'I am his lordship's butler.' (Pause.) 'I see.' (Pause.) 'Then I will fetch her ladyship.'

Rory rolled his eyes at me as he headed across the hall. I was acutely aware that the telephone remained on. Any noise I made could be heard down the line, so I remained as still as a statue. There was a whirring sound from the telephone. I eyed it warily. It didn't appear to be doing anything else.

Richenda clopped past me and gave an audible sniff of distain. She picked up the telephone. 'Y-yes,' she said. (Pause.) 'This is she.' (Pause.) 'You must be mistaken. She wrote to me herself. I am an old friend.' (Pause.) 'Can I speak to her Highness? What do you mean she is unavailable? I don't know who you think you are... Hallo? Hallo? McLeod! McLeod! This wretched thing is malfunctioning.'

Rory, who had somehow been there all along, took the receiver from Richenda and listened. 'They have ended the conversation, your ladyship.'

'Then you must get them back at once!'

'If you could tell me the number you wish to call I will endeavour to do so.'

'I have no idea. The exchange will have to find it. Euphemia, stop fiddling with those flowers and go away!'

The last two words were positively shouted. I

felt under the circumstances I need not curtsey and made as dignified an exit as I could to my parlour to check over the day's menus.

I was in the middle of trying to decipher whether Lady Stapleford, who had immediately taken over the duty of the daily menus, did wish a porridge of cauliflower with truffle sauce, which seemly highly unlikely, when all hell broke out across the hall. Richenda and Richard were screaming at each other in the hall. All I could hear was Richenda's demanding tones and Richard sounding steadfastly refusing.

A door slammed with finality and I guessed this was Richard retreating into his study. Richenda began to scream hysterically. She appeared to have a particularly well-developed set of lungs. Much as I would have loved to empty cold water over her I doubted it was my place. I heard the faint sound of the butler's parlour door closing. Rory had obviously decided to discreetly remove himself from the scene. Even the sounds of Mrs Deighton in her kitchen had ceased or were being eclipsed by the screaming. Richenda continued and the whole house waited.

I jumped at a tap on my door. Mr Bertram came in. 'Can't you do something?' he asked.

'How did you...?'

'I used the servants' stair.'

I suppressed a smile. 'She's your sister, sir.'

'Half-sister. And she's a female.'

'Sisters usually are.'

'Euphemia, I have no idea how to deal with Richenda in hysterics. I've never seen her do this before.'

'Much as I would like to slap Lady Richenda, I need to retain my position.'

'Only because you declined my proposal,' said Mr Bertram grimly.

'Honestly, this is really not the time.'

But Mr Bertram was using the opportunity of being in my room to cross the room and become far too close to my person for politeness sake.

'Euphemia, you can't prefer dealing with my family's whims to being my wife!'

'Please, I thought we had considered this subject closed.'

'Do you not care for me at all, Euphemia?'

'That isn't the point.'

Mr Bertram's face lit up. 'So you do?'

'Mr Bertram, this isn't fitting,' I said, placing my hands behind me and bracing myself against the chair back. 'I am a housekeeper.'

In the distance Richenda continued to scream. It was most distracting. I could not seem to be able to order my thoughts as I wished. The sole retort that kept coming to mind was the ridiculously, ludicrous, but you do not love me, when in truth all I needed to say was I was promised to another. Whatever else Mr Bertram might be, maddening, infuriating, and impulsive, he was most certainly a gentleman. But somehow I could not seem to form the right sentences.

Suddenly the screaming stopped. I felt as if someone had abruptly stopped beating my head with hammers. The relief was astounding. 'I should go and see what has happened,' I said and I pushed past him.

'I'm coming with you,' said Mr Bertram and I

could tell from his tone that nothing I said would make any difference. He was in his terrier-with-a-bone mood that I knew so well.

In the hall we found Richenda standing open mouthed with one hand pressed to a reddening cheek. In front of her, totally calm, was Lady Stapleford.

'How dare you hit me!' said Richenda.

'How dare you make such an inappropriate and unladylike a noise.' There was heavy emphasis on the 'unladylike'.

'She – she – isn't coming. I didn't even speak to her. It was her secretary. He hung up on me. I've – I've told everyone.' Then Richenda began to cry in earnest, wracking, noisy sobs. Some ladies cry well and even to advantage. Not Richenda Stapleford. Mr Bertram threw one alarmed look at his mother and turned tail and fled. I began to back quietly away.

'Miss St John, Miss Richenda requires hot tea and brandy. Immediately. In my boudoir. Bring it yourself.' And, grabbing Miss Richenda by an ample upper arm, Lady Stapleford towed her away.

I allowed some minutes to pass before I executed her commission. I had no desire to see Miss Richenda in such distress, not least because she would always resent me for it. So when I did enter the boudoir the scene was quieter. Lady Stapleford appeared to be on a long scolding diatribe the message of which was the always unwelcome *I told you so.*

Miss Richenda fairly gulped down her brandy. 'Fine. Fine. Stepmama, you were right. What do

I do?'

'Accept the situation with good grace.'

'But I can't. The Earl. The Court.'

'If I might make a suggestion,' came Suzette's voice in strained, mock-refined accents, 'am I right in understanding that no one you know has actually met this Highness person?' Miss Richenda nodded. 'Indeed, part of the coup was persuading her to come to England for the first time.'

'Then that's alright then,' said Suzette.

'What on earth can you mean?' asked Lady Stapleford.

'I reckons you could hire someone to play the part. Lord knows most of the time we're play-acting our way through the world.'

'What a nonsensical idea,' snapped Lady Stapleford.

'No,' said Miss Richenda, 'it might work.'

'Her Highness's people would deny it.'

Miss Richenda shook her head. 'I could arrange that they would neither deny or confirm.' She said slowly. 'Part of the reason she agreed was that I know something she did that summer which her parents certainly don't know.'

'Ooh,' said Suzette, 'do tell.'

'I don't know who it was,' said Richenda, 'but she had a lover.'

'Good heavens, Richenda,' said Lady Stapleford, 'you are playing with fire here.'

'I could write and say I quite understood her office's response, but...'

'Richenda, that is blackmail!'

'Reckon it would work though!' said Suzette,

64

her eyes bright. I knew her type. She didn't want to help out Miss Richenda as much as hold this new secret over her.

'But who could I get to do it?' said Richenda. 'It would have to be someone who wouldn't expose us ever.'

'Euphemia,' said Lady Stapleford.

'Perfect!' cried Miss Richenda.

Lady Stapleford stiffened, 'I was going to say, Euphemia, remove the tea tray.'

'At once, your ladyship.'

'Oh no you don't,' said Miss Richenda. 'She'd be perfect. Absolutely perfect.'

Chapter Nine

Play-acting

The argument raged over my head. I couldn't look anyone in the face. While I might not have royal blood in my veins, I knew that I was more of a lady by birth and breeding than anyone in the room. I was partly horrified by my situation and another part of me was almost hysterical at the ridiculous irony of it all.

Surprisingly enough Suzette argued hard in the favour of the scheme. 'She's hoity enough and with my skills I can make 'er look the part. Her own mother wouldn't recognise her when I've finished.'

'That wouldn't be a problem. No one on the

guest list except the family know Euphemia,' said Richenda.

'The visitors to the Highland Lodge,' I said quickly. 'They would know me.'

'And this above all else tells me the girl is not fit for such a charade,' said Lady Stapleford. She turned to me. 'Men do not look at the faces of servant girls.'

Suzette gave a little giggle. I felt a hot blush crawl across my skin. Richenda began to argue violently once more. The just of her argument was the social disgrace she would suffer if her chief bridesmaid did not appear.

'Enough,' said Lady Stapleford, raising her hand to her forehead. 'You are giving me a head. There is only one way to settle this argument.'

And so I found myself in the kitchen explaining to Mrs Deighton that there would be one more guest for dinner.

'Who?' asked Rory. 'I have not been notified of any planned arrivals today.'

'It'll be the dashing groom unable to keep from the side of his bride,' said Merry.

'Actually, it's me,' I said.

A stony silence greeted my announcement. Then Merry begun to laugh. 'Oh you had me there for a minute,' she said. 'I'll say this for you, Euphemia, you don't tell jokes often but when you do.'

I held up my hand. 'No, really. It's some mad idea of the ladies. I will be sitting down to dinner with the family. Merry, you will have to take over my role.'

Everyone began talking at once. Rory dealt

66

with the situation, by gesturing at the passage to the butler's pantry. I led the way.

'What is going on'?' he demanded.

'The chief bridesmaid Richenda has been boasting about to everyone is unable to come.'

'So she has decided to invite her housekeeper instead?' Rory's eyes were flinty hard.

'No, of course not. She wants me to pretend to be the lady concerned.'

'You cannot have agreed to such madness?'

'It was agree or lose my position. Besides, this dinner is a test. If I cannot comport myself properly here Richenda will have to give up her idea.'

Rory gripped me firmly on the upper arms. 'Are ye telling me the truth? This is no Mr Bertram trying to convince his family that you are worthy to be his wife?'

I broke away angrily. 'How could you think that after I had accepted your proposal?'

'Aye, well, a landed gent is a much better prospect than a butler.'

'I had my chance to marry him before.'

'And maybe you're regretting you did not take it.'

'If you think that then you don't know me at all!'

'Euphemia, I forbid you to get involved with this ridiculous scheme.'

'You forbid it! Who are you to forbid me?'

'Your affianced husband if you are to be believed.'

'No man, even my wedded husband, shall ever forbid my actions! My moral conscience is my guide.' And with that I flounced out of the room.

I regretted much as soon as I left. Not that I would ever allow any man to forbid me. My mother would say it is tiresomely fashionable of me, but I do not intend to ever be any man's chattel. But I regretted our argument. Richenda had put me in a terrible position and I would have welcomed Rory's support rather than his suspicion.

An hour with the sarcastic Suzette and a borrowed dress saw me ready to sit down to dinner. The men had been apprised of the plan. When I entered the drawing room. Sir Richard stared at me with his mouth open. Then he gave a bark of laughter. 'Good gad, sis. If I didn't know it was our starchy housekeeper I'd never have guessed. You've worked wonders.

'It was Stepmama's maid. For all her coarseness she is quite a wonder.'

I went and sat very correctly, back ramrod straight, on a small chair near the fire. Mr Bertram brought me a small glass of sherry. 'You look every inch a lady, Euphemia. Just as I knew you would.'

'Ah, there he goes again,' broke in Sir Richard, 'don't forget little brother, this is all a game. She isn't one of us and never will be.'

Bertram blushed and turned away from the group. 'Still got your claws into him, I see,' continued the hateful Sir Richard. 'Well, it won't do my girl. It won't do. Richenda's idea is a capital bit of fun for a dull evening, but there is no way one such as you could pass for a real lady.'

Oh the sins of vanity and pride! I had intended to make several mistakes at dinner to quash the plan. Nothing too obvious but social faux pas enough to ensure Lady Stapleford would insist the plan went no further, but Sir Richard had my blood up. That he, at best a countryman who pretended to be a gentleman, might suggest that I, with my connections, was unworthy, was intolerable.

I sincerely regret to say I made it through the entire dinner without once making a mistake. I did not rise to Sir Richard's ribbing. I pretended either to not hear or not understand unsavoury comments when they were made. I acted all in all as if this family of bankers and murderers was beneath my notice. I would have made my mother proud.

At the end of the meal, Lady Stapleford dismissed me. I walked slowly across the hall towards the stairs and Suzette, who would need to unpin and undress my costume, wondering what I had done. Rory stood waiting for me in the hall. I could not read his expression.

'You heard,' I said to him, 'you heard Richenda admit it was all her plan.'

'I did,' said Rory evenly. 'I also saw you. Your performance was flawless.'

'I am around the family every day. Some of it must have rubbed off.'

'I'll go further,' said Rory, 'your behaviour was the most ladylike in the room.'

I smiled and dropped a little curtsey. 'Why thank you, kind sir.'

No answering smile met mine. 'I always knew you were hiding something, Euphemia. I thought you'd tell me in your own time, but seeing you tonight I have to ask myself if I know you at all. What is it you haven't told me? If we are to be wed I need to know the truth.'

I looked his straight in the eye. 'I cannot tell you the whole of it, but I am related – distantly related – to people who might be deemed aristocratic by some.'

'How aristocratic?'

'I told you my father was a vicar. That is true. My mother,' I hesitated, 'my mother is connected to an important family, but there was an argument a long time ago, and the connection was broken.'

'So you are a lady?'

'I am a vicar's daughter. Nothing more.'

'Bertram, does he know this?'

I shook my head. 'The only people who know are my mother, my little brother and you.'

'Well, that's something,' said Rory. 'But when I saw you sitting with them you looked more at home than I have ever seen you among the servants.'

I put my hand on his chest. 'I can assure you that every moment I was sitting there I was wishing I was with you all at the kitchen table.'

Rory bowed his head and covered my hand with his. 'I do believe you, Euphemia, but we all are what we are. Blood will out. If you love me give up this scheme. It can only lead to trouble.'

'But if I do them this favour they will be in my debt. They will have to agree to let us marry.'

'You've said it yourself many a time the Staplefords will do what they want. We are nothing to them.'

'But...'

'Give it up, Euphemia. I beg you. If you love me give it up.'

70

Chapter Ten

The Court

I could find no way to do what Rory wanted. I even made so bold as to suggest to Richenda that she use her knowledge of her royal friend to make her agree to come.

'That only shows how much you have to learn,' said Miss Richenda scornfully. 'My friend could never explain to her parents that she had a lover, but she could choose without repercussion to instruct her staff not to contradict any reports of her presence for the sake of not embarrassing an old friend.'

'It won't work,' I said.

'Stepmama will be giving you lessons every day until we depart for The Court. I have sent to London for clothes for you. Suzette will act as your maid. I shall take Merry with us as mine. Everything will go well.'

'But the servants...'

'Want to keep their positions. Accept it, Euphemia. For a short period in your dull, little life you will get to play at being a lady. You will always have those memories.'

'Your brother...'

'Thinks this is a great laugh and, before you ask, Tippy will do whatever I ask.'

I was trapped. I could see no way out. Like

Rory I had a deep foreboding this would not end well. Though I could never have suspected what was to happen.

We arrived at The Court on a sharp summer morning that carried the breath of autumn on the wind. It was late in the afternoon and four days before the wedding. Dinners and rehearsals would take up the next three days.

'The Court' is, naturally, not its full name, but were I to give the rest of it many people who might wish to remain anonymous in these pages would be exposed. However, for the sake of readers less familiar with the naming conventions of the English great houses, let me assure you that The Court has nothing to do with the Royal Court. It is simply a familiar abbreviation of the house's name – for example it could have been Dently Court or some such thing. By dropping the identifying name it is implied everyone in the conversation knows where it is and if you don't then you shouldn't be part of the conversation in the first place. The upper classes do love their nicknames. After all nicknames are one of the very best ways to exclude the socially inferior. By this I don't mean the servants, for the true aristocrat cares nothing for his servants' opinions, but that awful growing group that is beginning to be known as the middle classes. The Staplefords before the award of their peerage were most definitely middle-class. Of course they knew this, and were among the most vehement in their hatred of the middle classes. But really, I fear I am becoming most radical. I apologise.

In our little motorcade the family was all

present. Merry came as lady's maid and Rory as valet. None of the other servants the Staplefords had could be trusted with the full secret of my impostor charade and, perhaps more importantly, none of the others knew how to behave in such a grand establishment.

As the motor entered the final stretch of the tree-lined drive, I saw Richenda blanch, and even Lady Stapleford appeared a little white about the mouth. I saw an Earl's residence, much like the one my mother had grown up in as a girl. Before us lay a big sprawling house that needed hordes of servants to keep it working, and a building strictly divided by the green baize door. The life upstairs of the betters and the army of lowers working downstairs. The whole structure was like a giant swan with the aristocratic members living a life of ease and leisure and the servants working like devils from dawn to dusk to make their master's world a better place.

However, it did have a very pretty portico.

The great house threw us into shadow as the car drew up. It was cold enough to make me wish I had chosen a winter dress. Some of the senior servants were lined up along the steps; after all. Richenda was joining the family, even if she would only be the Earl's great-niece by marriage.

The lady in question looked decidedly green around the gills. 'There is a question of pre-science,' hissed Lady Stapleford. 'As bride-to-be, Richenda, you must go first and I will follow.'

'Actually, we can't do that,' I said. 'If I am a member of a Royal family, even a European one, then I outrank both of you.'

The colour came back into the cheeks of Lady Stapleford and her lips parted to no doubt utter a scalding response, but the butler was already at my door. He opened it and extended his hand. I gave it to him and he bowed very low. 'Your Highness, welcome to The Court.'

'Thank you,' I said, inclining my head a fraction. I descended gracefully and for the first time in my life felt grateful to my mother for the hours of deportment she had made me practice.

'Indeed you are most welcome, my dear,' said an elderly lady dressed in the very best fashion. This must be the Countess. No one else would dare be so informal with royalty. I decided to be gracious.

'Thank you,' I said. 'You have a lovely house. It reminds me of one of our smaller winter palaces.'

I heard a gasp of horror from Lady Stapleford behind me, but the Countess looked at me with a twinkle her eyes. 'Shall we let Robbins see to your luggage? I shall take you up myself.'

This, naturally enough, elected a gasp from Richenda, who had expected the Countess's undivided attention. However, the rest of the family were left to the housekeeper, a Mrs Merion, while the Countess escorted me to my very large bedchamber and dressing room, apologizing frequently for the coldness of the house and the 'rather temperamental' hot water system.

I assured her that the house was very lovely, my room extremely tasteful and if she could send my maid and a cup of tea up to me I would like a little time to recover from my journey before predinner drinks.

Nothing seemed too much and I had barely taken off my outer clothing before there was a tap at the door and Merry appeared carrying a tea tray. She closed the door behind her, carefully supporting the tray with one hand and made her way to an occasional table. Once she had set her burden down she collapsed onto the floor, her fist stuffed into her mouth, as she attempted to stifle the gales of laughter that over took her. Tears of pure joy ran down her face. I poured myself a cup of tea and waited for her to recover herself.

Eventually Merry sat up and wiped her tears with the edge of her skirt. 'I'm sorry,' she gulped, 'but you should have seen Lady Stapleford's face when the Earless greeted you first! And then Richenda nearly had a cow when you said the house was small.'

'Countess,' I said. 'Not Earless.'

Merry staggered to her feet and dropped me what she obviously thought was a deep curtsey, but looked unfortunately vulgar. 'I am so sorry, Your 'ighness.' This set her off again. Although this time she managed to attain the dignity of sitting on a small sofa rather than rolling around on the floor.

'Merry,' I said seriously, 'you're right this whole escape is laughable. But it's also very dangerous. I said what I did about the Court because the Countess didn't give me my title. We were establishing our respective social standings. If I'd got that wrong I could have been exposed as a fraud.'

'What?'

'What the Staplefords don't understand is that

every conversation I have here will be watched and analysed.'

'You mean they are suspicious?'

'I mean because the English are always sensitive about foreign royalty. They assume all other Royals are not as important as their own, but they are never quite sure where to put us in the social ranking when we visit.'

''Ow do you know all this?' asked Merry, her head on one side. 'Cos the way it looked when we arrived only you knew what to do.'

'That's how it should be.'

'No, you don't,' said Merry. 'Don't dodge the question.'

I sighed. 'You know my father was a Vicar. Sometimes he had to visit the Archbishop's Palace and there could be important visitors there.'

'The Archbishop had a palace?'

I waved this comment aside. 'It's just what the residence of a bishop is called. Most of them look nothing like palaces. Anyway Pa got one of these books on etiquette in case he ever met anyone important. I read it. That's all.'

'But the Staplefords hadn't a clue.'

'I'm sure they don't think they are in need of reading etiquette books.'

'Looks to me like they are,' said Merry watching me very closely.

'I don't care if they make mistakes,' I said. 'I mustn't. I'm not sure that what I'm doing isn't illegal.'

'Then why are you doing it? They're tripling my wages for the time here. That's my reason. What's yours?'

76

'You got a much better deal than me. They said they would fire me if I didn't do it.'

'Blimey,' said Merry, 'they really don't like you, do they?'

'Something to do with trying to get Lord Stapleford hanged for murder, I expect.'

'That and seducing the younger son of the house.'

'Merry!' I cried. 'I have never seduced anyone.'

'Yeah, I know,' said Merry. 'You've never been one to take advantage of your position like a proper servant would. But you can't deny Mr Bertram isn't sweet on you.'

'Honestly, I think Bertram's feelings for me swing between intense annoyance and mild affection.'

'I've seen the intense annoyance,' said Merry with a grin. 'Now come here, I've got to re-pin all your bloody hair for dinner.'

'I have to have a bath first and change my dress and jewellery.'

'Lord, what a bloody palaver!' said Merry. 'I'll be glad when this is all over.' I couldn't help but heartily agree.

Chapter Eleven

Polite Conversation Before Dinner

I doubt there are more dangerous situations than the English pre-dinner drinks. It is a time when reputations can be shredded, alliances forged or severed and all over a sweet sherry.

None of the Staplefords had thought to collect me from my chambers, so when the gong went I made my way down the huge marble staircase trusting the noise of social exchange would guide me. The company was standing in the large entrance hall. On all sides ran a minstrel's gallery and the hall itself was the full height of the building. The gaping maw of a fireplace had been banked up with a small forest, but the warmth had not spread and the company were gently jostling for places close to the fire. Their voice mostly high pitched and nasal echoed unpleasantly. A frequent braying laugh betrayed Tippy's presence. As I descended I saw him with his arm around Richenda's waist talking to the Earl. A break in the conversation unfortunately carried Tippy's comment up to echo in the hall, 'I'm her birthday night surprise,' he said and brayed again. The Earl's face became even more stony. He looked much like a hawk who thinks he is swooping down upon a tasty rabbit, only to discover that it is an inedible toad.

'He's not doing himself any favours, is he?' said a soft voice at my elbow. The voice had a faint West Country burr. I caught my breath and then turned to see Mr Fitzroy looking down at me. He was dressed a great deal more smartly than he had been in the Highlands when we had last met, but there remained something neat, tidy and forgettable about his entire appearance. He gave me a slight, wry smile. 'Allow me to escort you over to the drinks,' he said and offered me his arm.

'Sir, have we met?' I said in crisp English, but a low voice.

Fitzroy's answer was even softer. 'Don't be foolish, Euphemia Martins.' I slid my arm through his and allowed him to escort me to a silent, stiff servant, who was holding out a drinks tray. He picked up one for us both and led me towards the window. We were now a little way away from the nearest guests, but clearly in sight of the whole hall.

'I suppose if anyone would see through my disguise it would be you,' I said taking my drink from him. 'What do you propose to do?'

'You mean will I give you up?'

'Yes,' I said swallowing and nodding slightly at a gentleman with a monocle.

'You're keeping remarkably calm,' said Fitzroy maddeningly. 'Tell me there is more to this charade than Richenda Stapleford's pride?'

I gritted my teeth. 'There is the small matter of keeping my position.'

'I am disappointed,' said Fitzroy, turning slightly to stare out of the window behind us.

'So?'

'If you had done your homework you would know that the lady you are misrepresenting and I have a history.'

'This is a Stapleford plan,' I said acidly. 'Do you think they would have thought things through.'

Fitzroy frowned. 'Do you recognise anyone in this room. No, don't look round, use the reflection.'

'Apart from the Staplefords I now recognise the Earl and his Countess, Tipton, and that looks like Muller, but I doubt I know him in my new persona.'

'You are very ill-prepared.'

'I know.'

'I doubt I will need to give you up. You'll do that yourself in a matter of moments.'

'If anyone here has previously met the lady I am misrepresenting then I am lost.'

'Of course,' said Fitzroy. 'But she will have heard of many of the people here.'

'Really?' I asked, arching my eyebrow in a distinctly aristocratic manner.

Fitzroy gave a low laugh. 'She will have heard of Tipton's elder brother. He's over by the fireplace. The tallest man. He's known as Tip-Top among the upper classes, and not ironically.'

'And he's related to Baggy Tipton?' I asked astonished.

'I'm here to recruit him. Lots of charm, bored with society and not enough money. All areas I can work with.'

'Why are you telling me all this?'

'I am trying to make conversation,' said Fitzroy,

'and I am not in the habit of doing that with people who know what I am.'

'But why?'

'My dear girl, I am doing you a favour. I am well aware that the only way Richenda could ensure that the lady in question did not deny that she was ever present would be if she knew her secret.'

'This has all been very interesting,' I said, 'but I think I should circulate before your exclusive attention attracts rumours.'

'But that is what I am telling you, my dear. You and I are lovers.'

'W-w-what?' I gasped.

'I was sent on a mission to gather information about certain areas of her country's industry. Let's just say I got rather more than that.'

I could feel myself blushing horribly.

'Excellent,' continued Fitzroy. 'Those in the know will certainly believe now you are who you say you are. Shall I expect you at midnight?'

'No, you will not,' I hissed.

Fitzroy chuckled. 'You need to learn how to embrace your part.' He turned away from me and caught the eye of an elder man, who came across to us. 'My lady allow me to present the Earl of...'

As he uttered that last word I felt my world rock. The man standing in front of me was no other than my grandfather.

I fled.

Chapter Twelve

An Interesting Night

Or I would have fled if Fitzroy's fingers hadn't pinched my elbow hard and held me back. I tried to focus on what my relative was saying '...so if you would be so gracious as to allow me to escort you into dinner, your Highness. I'm afraid old Ratty rather feels he has to take in the bride-to-be. I appreciate she is a friend of yours, but she does seem to rather want a bit of a show, what?'

Your Highness. He had no idea who I was.

I heard my voice answering. 'Of course not. I should be delighted to accompany you in to dinner.'

My grandfather smiled and his face changed, softened. His whole visage was etched with lines and he had the deep complexion of one who had spent much of his life outdoors. He also had a very bristly moustache. I could see the echo of mother in his features. Thank you, my de- your Highness. It will make everything much easier. I shall try very hard not to be too boring an old duffer.'

'I'm sure you could never be that,' I said. My mind was racing. Could this be my opportunity to discover why my grandfather still refused to acknowledge my mother, even though she was now widowed and thus free from the connection he despised?

Mr Fitzroy bowed and withdrew. 'Very charming man, that Lord Milford,' said my grandfather. 'Always thought there was something a bit cavey about him.' He caught himself up with a cough. 'My apologies. My wife used to be a terrible gossip and now she's gone I seem rather to have taken up her role. That's one of the problems of getting old, you don't get to do things so much. Too creaky in the joints. You end up watching people, don't you know.'

'It certainly is a mixed party,' I said looking around the room and silently absorbing the name Fitzroy was using. Could that be his real name?

'You can say that again. Ratty didn't want to hold the wedding here, but it seems that Baggy just wouldn't let go. Like a terrier with a rat, he said, just kept banging on and on about until Ratty felt it would be easier to let him have it and get the whole thing over with.'

'Ratty?'

'The Earl.'

'Of course, you English do love your nicknames,' I said.

'We do indeed,' said my grandfather. 'Not that the younger generation seem to come up with anything very imaginative, Tip-Top, Baggy, the Nag.' He coughed again and ran his fingers through his moustache. 'Err-umm.'

'The Nag?' I caught sight of Richenda smiling broadly and showing large teeth in her very long face. 'Richenda Stapleford?'

'She does tend to go on a bit about women's rights and all that palaver,' said my grandfather apologetically.

'Nothing to do with her appearance?' I asked.

My grandfather fairly snorted into his drink. 'I can tell we are going to get on, you and I,' he said and gave me a sly wink.

I smiled, but mentally I was reeling. This was the man who had been painted as an ogre to me all my life? This gossipy, friendly old man?

The dinner gong sounded and we all processed into the grand dining room. A full thirty places were set out at the table. Although the Court had gas lighting, the table had been lit with several candelabras. Crystal and silver reflected the warm yellow flames. Small delicate arrangements of flowers lined the centre of the table at exactly the right height so one could still see across the table. Not that one would talk to the person opposite at such an event. Conversation was on a side to side basis and strictly rotational. I waited to see who I would be seated next to apart from my grandfather.

'Renard Layfette,' said a well-dressed man in his thirties. 'I am a distant cousin of the Staplefords. Richenda will have mentioned me.'

'I don't believe so,' I said carefully. Renard certainly bore the self-important air that all the Staplefords had. Dark-haired, like Bertram, I could see a family resemblance. 'You are related to the second Lady Stapleford?'

'Is not everyone related to everyone in our world?' he said with a small wave of his hand. I detected a slight French accent this time, but really his English was excellent. I told him so.

'I was raised to speak several languages at home,' he said with a shrug. 'It has been useful. I

84

travel a lot.'

My grandfather's attention seemed to have been captured by the woman on the other side. She was small, stout and talking twenty to the dozen in a hurried undertones.

'You like to travel?' I asked my other dinner companion, who had not referred once to my status though he must have known.

Again came the little shrug and a world weary sigh. 'It has been necessary.'

The soup arrived. It lay clear and brownish in the insignia stamped dish. No doubt it was highly fashionable. It smelled of fish and sprouts. I took a tentative sip. It tasted worse than it looked.

'The English,' said Renard with yet another shrug. 'They cannot cook.'

'I have had many good meals in the homes of my English friends,' I said, forgetting for a moment that this was meant to be my first time in the country.

'Cooked by a French cook, no doubt. Some hostesses are rightly proud of their French cooks. Others try to pretend it is an ordinary chef, but always if the food is good it will be a Frenchman cooking.'

The footman removed my soup. He did not even bother asking if I had finished, but I thought I detected a commiserating demeanour.

The voice of the woman on the other side of my grandfather floated over to me. 'Honestly, Gregory, I thought we'd never find a woman to take him on, let alone a lady. No one can accuse me of being a doting mother. I know my sons. Tip-top's the best of them, but little Baggy has always been the runt of the litter, poor chap. No surprise he turned out like he did. At least she has money. I hate to think what their offspring will look like. Ugly buggers I imagine.'

On my other side Renard sniggered. 'That is Amelia Tipton. Mother of the groom. Apparently she blames the loss of her figure on her third son. In her day she was accounted a great beauty, if you can believe that. Now she is more dumpy duck than woman. But I do not know why she calls him Baggy.'

'Apparently it is the custom at English boarding schools to de-bag or remove the trousers of some-one one dislikes or who has been found to be wanting in some way. A quaint boyish custom,' I said.

'I can imagine that the groom often found himself in such a position,' said Renard. 'It is unfair when nature gifts a man with more ambition than sense.'

Really, I wondered, did no one here have anything good to say about anyone else? Was this the high society that my mother had so longer for and that she was desperate to thrust my little brother and me into? Next time we met I would tell her frankly I wanted no part of it. There was nothing jolly or celebratory about this meal. The sole aim of all here appeared to be to get a shot off at one another.

I let my eyes drift down the table. I saw Lord Milford/Fitzroy chatting to a young woman, who was blushing deeply. Wouldn't the Staplefords recognise him as Fitzroy? It appeared not. If I hadn't declared himself to me, would I have known? He had a very forgettable face.

Bertram had been placed next to an aging dowager, who kept putting up her hand to her ear and bending so far her clothing dangled in her soup. I surmised she was deaf as a post. Bertram certainly wore an expression of frustration.

Lady Stapleford had managed to get herself seated on one side of the Earl at the head of the table. She smiled a lot and turned a head in a marked manner as if deep in thought. I guessed she was attempting to show her best side. I acquitted her of thinking. Richard Stapleford was ignoring his dinner companions and drinking deeply. Richenda, seated opposite Tippy, attempted to flirt through the foliage with nauseating effect. And still the courses continued, each worse than the last. This caused Renard to sniff and chuckle smugly. He began to declaim all the ills of English society, apparently believing that as a foreigner I would agree.

After what seemed an age, the Countess stood giving the signal for the ladies to retire to the drawing room for tea. The men stayed behind for port and cigars.

I managed to catch the Countess on the way to the tea, and pleading fatigue, excuse myself from what no doubt would be a vicious round of polite gossip.

My bed called to me. All I wanted to do was lie down and sleep. Of course, as with all the simplest of my desires it was not to be.

Chapter Thirteen

Ambushed

I had barely opened the door of my chamber before Merry rushed towards me. She started grabbing pins from my hair before I had even sat down.

'Where on earth have you been?' she squeaked. 'I've been waiting ages for you and I've got to do Miss Richenda and Lady Stapleford next.'

'They are still downstairs having tea. I doubt they will be up for a while.'

Merry slowed her frantic pace. 'Honestly?'

'It's not like Stapleford Hall,' I said, 'there is a trifle more to occupy the guests here. Mostly by being mean to each other.'

Merry slumped down on the bed. 'So I'm going to be up half the night waiting for them and still expected to be up early?' I nodded. 'And here was me thinking coming to this big fancy house was going to be fun. It's all right for you play-acting at being one of the nobs.'

'I can assure you I'm not enjoying the experience.'

'Shouldn't that be one is not enjoying the experience?' I threw a hairbrush at her. Merry dodged. 'Miss Richenda's done that once too often to me for you to catch me out. She's being right temperamental at the moment.'

88

'Has she said where she will be living after the wedding?'

'Well that's the thing,' said Merry picking up a discarded cushion and making herself comfortable. 'She wants to go back to Stapleford Hall. Tippy wants her to go home with him to the Tipton seat, wherever that is, but she hates his mother.'

'From what I saw I can't imagine anyone liking Amelia Tipton much. She called Tippy the runt of the litter.'

'Well, toffs is funny about children. It's not like they raise them themselves. It's all wet-nurses and nannies and boarding schools. And besides he is a bit of a runt. I bet Richenda will squish him to pieces on their wedding night. Either that or he'll have to climb...'

I stuck my fingers in my ears and began to hum. Merry pulled my hands away. 'All right. It's not like you to be squeamish.'

'You've certainly come a long way since you were fond of George Layfette.'

Merry tossed her head. 'That was a silly crush. Merrit and I, we are very serious. We both like looking at views,' she added ambiguously.

'Merry, you haven't?' I said startled.

'Even if I had what business would be it of yours?' Her face flushed and she bit her lip, but she kept her chin up. I could have said something about her being a maid in my care as housekeeper, but I suspected that would only make her withdraw further. So I just said, 'Be careful, Merry.'

'Anyway,' said Merry picking up the previous thread of our conversation as if nothing had happened, 'the real issue is where Lady Stapleford is going to live. For what I can gather the late Sir Richard didn't leave her much. He wanted it all to go to his eldest son and she thinks he thought she'd leave anything she had to Bertram.'

'You mean she's destitute?'

'Nothing as bad as that. But Suzette says she's been going through the money at a fair old rate. She wants to live like she thinks a lady should, but she's not got the budget. So now she's thinking of basing herself at Stapleford Hall and none of the children want that.'

'Are you and Suzette friendly?' I asked surprised.

'Not friendly like you and me, but we rub along okay. She's been showing me how to do hair more fashionably. Reckons I could train to be a lady's maid for real and not just when we're short on staff.'

'I'd miss you,' I said seriously.

'Well, I was thinking how Richenda doesn't have a proper lady's maid and I don't think her mother will put up with sharing Suzette for long.'

'Do you think Suzette will stay with Lady Stapleford if she chooses to stay at Stapleford Hall. There's nothing going on in the country.'

Merry nodded. 'I wondered about that. But she said how she was very grateful to Lady Stapleford and would be happy to stay with her. I reckon she thinks her ladyship will start doing the rounds of weekends away, so she won't have to stay at the Hall all the time.'

'Why would she do that? She's never been interested in visiting around the country before.'

'I think that might have been more the late Lord Stapleford. With the hours he worked weekends away weren't possible. Besides she's been widowed a decent time now. She'll be thinking of marrying again. It's the only way she's ever going to improve her situation.'

I reached up to unfasten my necklace; one lent to me by Lady Stapleford. I was surprised to find I was feeling sorry for her. She was a vain, arrogant, dislikeable woman, but she had been left in poor circumstances by a man who must not have cared for her very much. 'Do you know why Lord Stapleford married her?' I asked.

Merry giggled. 'You mean because it couldn't have been for love? I think she was meant to add a bit of class to the family. She had aristocratic French connections. George Layfette was related to some posh folks.'

'I thought he was related to the first Lady Stapleford.'

'That lot is all related to one another somehow,' said Merry shrugging. 'They've got their own little world and we've got ours. Only ours is bigger, dirtier and more difficult to live in.'

'There's a Renard Layfette here,' I said musingly. 'I wonder which side he's related to. I thought he looked a bit like Bertram.'

Merry's mouth fell open. 'Renard, here?' she said. 'Gawd almighty, that'll put the cat among the ruddy pigeons.'

'What do you mean?'

'He's the what-do-you-call-it, the black cow of the family.'

'Black sheep?' I suggested.

'Black something or other. All I know is that Lord Stapleford banished him from Stapleford Hall. He's been living abroad, or so George told me, and he made it sound as if he's been earning his way not quite in the normal manner.'

'Like what?'

'I don't know. George said it was too much for my tender young ears, which means either he didn't know or it was something bad. Lady Stapleford wouldn't even have his name mentioned in her presence. She took against him so much I wondered if there had been something a bit – you know – between them.'

'But he's the same age as Richard!'

'No.' Merry shook her head. 'He's about ten years older than that. In his forties, and Lady Stapleford will only own to be being in her late forties herself. Claims she was a child bride.'

I heard a light tap on the door. Suzette came in. 'Any sign of their ladyships coming up?' she said.

Merry looked at the clock over the mantel. 'Lord, we've been gassing on for ages.'

'There's a church rehearsal tomorrow,' said Suzette, 'so everyone will want to be up early.'

'Good grief,' I snapped, 'how on earth do they intend to keep up this charade if they don't tell me anything.'

'Well, I've just told you, haven't I?' said Suzette. 'Ten o'clock at the church. The motors will be waiting to take you across at quarter to.'

'Can I assume this message hasn't been somewhat delayed in reaching me?' I asked frostily.'

Suzette dropped a wonky curtsey, 'So sorry, your jumped up highness.'

92

There was a rap on the door. It didn't open. I gestured to Merry, who opened the door a crack. Baggy Tipton stood there. 'Where's your mistress?' he asked.

He caught sight of me behind Merry. Suzette had backed silently into a corner. 'Mr Tipton,' I said, 'this is most unseemly.'

Baggy Tipton elbowed Merry out of the way and stuck his head through the door. 'Just wanted to say,' he said in the loud whisper of a very drunk man, 'that you're doing splendidly and no one suspects a thing.'

'Go away,' said Merry, pushing him sharply in the ribcage. 'You'll ruin everything.'

'My, you're a sparky little thing. Want to come keep my bed warm on my last night of freedom, what?'

'No,' said Merry, as she managed to shove him through the door frame. She slammed the door in his face.

'I'm in the West Garden Room if you change your mind,' shouted Tipton far too loudly for comfort.

'If I ain't almost sorry for Richenda,' said Merry, leaning her back against the door and folding her arms. 'What's the matter with you? You look like you've seen a ghost.'

I turned to see Suzette had gone very white. 'Are you well?' I asked.

'I'm fine,' she snapped. 'First time I've seen Miss Richenda's new husband to be. Bit of a runt, isn't he?'

'His mother would certainly agree with you,' I said under my breath.

This time no one knocked. Lady Stapleford strode into the room. 'I should have known I would find you here gossiping. The lower classes always gravitate to each other,' she said with a nod in my direction. 'Suzette, I need you and Merry go and help my step daughter, she has a big day ahead of her.'

'But I've not finished with Euphemia,' said Merry casting an anxious look at my complicated evening dress.

'Well, you should have thought of that before. Shoo! Both of you, out of here.'

She turned to me. 'I see we can put you in fine clothes, but you will always revert to your own type. We shall see what my son has to say about this.'

She turned on her heel and with only a very slight wobble to suggest that she hadn't only been drinking tea, she left. The door closed with a click behind her. Ladies, as my mother, had taught me, do not slam doors even when unreasonably provoked.

I hoped Merry would return later to help me, but as the hands of the clock marched forward, no one came. I began the unequal struggle of a lady trying to rid herself of her vestments without her maid.

Well, I do not think the dress was greatly torn, and besides, I would not be wearing it again at The Court, or anywhere else for that matter. The Staplefords would just have to put up with the damage.

I found the last of my hairpins when I laid my head upon the pillow. I pulled it out, noting blood

94

on my finger and flung it petulantly across the room. No doubt it would stick in my foot later. Enough was enough. If I was to play the lady then play the lady I would. I rang my bell long and hard.

After far too long, Merry arrived at my door breathless and wide eyed. 'You'd better come,' she said urgently, 'there's all hell breaking loose out here. Lady Stapleford and Richenda are having a right cat fight.'

Chapter Fourteen

A Breakfast Never to be Forgotten

I stared open mouthed at Merry. A scream echoed down the hallway. 'C'mon,' shouted Merry and ran off. I scrambled out from under the heavy bedclothes and into a dressing gown. More shouts and screams came from the open doorway. I wasted precious time untangling my tassels and tying them properly. A lady would never let the world see her nightdress. My fingers were annoyingly clumsy as I rushed. All I could think was please, please, don't let there be another murder. I can't face another death. I can't. I can't.

Finally fit to be seen I dashed out into the corridor only to see Lady Stapleford and Richenda exit into their own rooms slamming their doors loudly.

Hesitantly, I went to Richenda's door and tapped. 'Are you alright?' Loud sobs were my only answer. I tapped again. Merry answered the door. She slipped out. 'You're too late,' she said.

'What was it all about?'

'I have no idea,' said Merry. 'But when Richenda decided to threaten her stepmother with a poker I thought I should get you.'

'Did she strike her?' I asked in horror. There was no sound coming from behind Lady Stapleford's door.

Merry shook her head. 'Suzette got it off her. Got right between them like she was breaking up a fight in a pub. I don't know what would have happened if she hadn't.'

'But you must have heard what it was about,' I insisted.

'I was coming back upstairs with Richenda's evening cocoa. She hadn't liked the way the housemaid had done it. They were already at it by the time I got back. Richenda was shouting something about Lady Stapleford being a liar and how she wasn't her real mother. By that point Lady Stapleford was in full retreat. When Richenda loses it, she really loses it.'

'You should get back to her,' I said. 'We're lucky we haven't had the whole house up here by now.'

Merry nodded and slipped inside. I made my way quickly back to my room. I tripped over a cup of cocoa that had been left outside my door. It splashed across the ivory and blue carpet. I kicked it again and went in and shut the door. Within minutes of laying my head on my pillow I was asleep.

I awoke to the sound of birds calling and sunlight on my face. A small figure was laying a fire in the grate. I sat up. The morning air rested cold against my face.

'Ooh, sorry, your miss-ship. I didn't mean to wake you,' said a small blonde maid. Her features were fine and bird-like. She peered over the end of the bed at me rather like a robin caught by a gardener. I guessed she was no more than fourteen years old.

'What time is it?'

'Not quite time for morning tea. If you were wanting it, your miss-ship.'

I was about to refuse when it occurred to me that no one had ever brought me tea in bed. 'That would be nice,' I said instead.

'Lucy'll be up with the trays in a short bit. I could go and hurry her if you like?'

I shook my head. 'I don't want to get you into trouble for waking me. What's your name?'

'Daisy.'

'We have a Daisy...' I stopped myself just in time, 'at the summer palace.'

'Ooo-er, wait till I tell me mum. She'll be right impressed.'

I couldn't think of a reply to this, so I lay back down. It felt very odd and distinctly uncomfortable to be resting while a child worked on readying my room. But she was good at her job and within a few moments I heard the crackle of flames bursting into life. I sat up once more. 'Is this house cold all year round?'

'Pretty much,' said Daisy. 'It's the old stones, that's what Mrs Merion says. They spend all winter soaking up the cold and damp and then eke it out over the summer. We're right in the open, but this place never seems to soak up the sun.'

'Is it a good place to work?'

'Don't right know, your miss-ship,' said Daisy with engaging candour. 'I never worked nowhere else. My mum says I was lucky to get taken on at a great house 'cos there's always opportunities for rising. Seeing as how in this many staff there's always ones that die – natural like.'

'Natural attrition.'

'Don't know nothing about that your miss-ship. Shall I go see if Lucy's done your tea yet?'

'Thank you.'

'She's meant to knock and bring it in like, but she's a bit scared of you. Thought you'd be right stuck up. I'll let her know you're a good 'un.'

My new best friend picked up her basket of kindling. ''Course, now you're awake, you might want to head down to breakfast. It's a serve-yourself in the dining room. Cook's made loads of dishes right from scrambled egg through to smoked 'addock. Though I 'ave to say that fish fair stinks. It must taste something wonderful for people to want to eat it.'

'Thank you. I'll ring for my maid.'

'Right you are, your miss-ship. I'll be seeing you tomorrow morning.'

Merry arrived fresh and alert. 'It's fair wonderful, the servants' quarters here,' she said. 'We're in an entire different building. There's a corridor between here and there. Mr Robbins, the butler, locks it at night and then it's just the servants. It don't half feel a relief.'

'To be separated from me?'

'Nah, get away with you. It's just Robbins stays

98

on in the big house and Mrs Merion's not that strict. It's quite informal and friendly over there.'

'That explains Daisy,' I said.

'Who?'

'The chatty girl who laid my fire.'

'Oooh, she'd get into trouble for talking to you. Might even lose her position.'

'I have no intention of telling on her. But I'd be grateful if you could persuade Daisy that I'm not her new best friend. She comes in very early.'

Merry giggled. 'Overdo the wine, did we, milady?'

I struggled out of bed. 'No, the food. It was terrible and there was far too much of it.'

'Which is why you're so eager to get to breakfast?'

'How's Rory?'

'Hmm.' Merry's face darkened. 'A bit like a bear with a sore head. He doesn't like the informality over there in the servants' quarters, but if you ask me what's really got his goat is that you are on the other side of the door. He's gone all broody like.'

'Oh dear,' I said.

'I reckon he's sweet on you. He's a good man. Now I've got my Merrit we could have a double wedding. Think of it – me and a highness getting married in the same ceremony!'

I threw a cushion at Merry. She dodged easily. Pulling out a morning dress from the wardrobe she said, 'Would this suit madam? It will bring out madam's eyes.'

'Oh, shut up,' I said and went to sluice water over my face at the night stand.

Suitably attired I made my way down to breakfast. There were two men I didn't recognise sitting at one end of the table. At the other Bertram sat alone. I took a plate from the hot stand and inspected the dishes under their silver covers. Daisy had been right; there was every form of breakfast food I could think of present. It also appeared to be well cooked. I helped myself to some herb-flavoured scrambled eggs, a small piece of smoked salmon and signalled to the butler to bring me some fresh black coffee. I sat down as near as propriety allowed to Bertram. He blinked at me with heavy eyes.

'Did you have a good evening?' I asked.

'You must be joking. They were going at it hammer and tongs.'

'I didn't see you there,' I said surprised.

'I don't know who saw them, but the whole ruddy house must have heard them.'

'I admit I was surprised. I knew there was no great liking between them,' I said, 'but to argue openly and in public seems out of character.'

'Out of character? You, of all people, should know their tempers. You saw what he did to Daisy.'

'Daisy?' I said, thinking of my new little friend. 'What has she got to do with it?'

'Tipton struck her across the face, remember? Just because he said the shaving water was cold.'

'Oh that Daisy. Not Daisy here,' I said. 'But we were speaking of your mother.'

'Are you sure you didn't overdo it on the sherry last night?' said Bertram. 'You're not making any sense. What are you talking about?'

'I'm talking about the row your mother and stepsister had last night.'

'What?' said Bertram.

'What are you talking about?'

'I'm talking about Richard and Tipton coming to blows last night. Tipton's going to have a shiner this morning.'

'But I saw him last night. He looked into my room to assure me I was doing well. He seemed tipsy, but not upset.'

'Must have been before he came downstairs again. What's this about my mother and Richenda.'

To save further confusion I summarised briefly what I had witnessed between the two women last night. Bertram shrugged. 'Women get so tense before weddings. If I'm honest I suspect Mama rather wants her own wedding. She's not fit to live alone.'

'You wouldn't object to her remarrying?' I asked curiously.

'Replacing my *beloved* father, you mean?' said Bertram. 'Well, he wasn't, and if she does it'll mean there's less likelihood of her trying to live with me.'

'Happy families all round.' I sighed. 'So what's up between Richard and Tipton?'

'Money I expect. Under my father's will Richenda's money transfers to her husband on her marriage. I think Richard thought he had Tipton under his thumb.'

'But last night the worm was doing some turning?'

'Exactly,' said Bertram. 'He is pretty buoyed up being at the Court and hobnobbing with his posh relations. He was digging at Richard about how he didn't have any and the only thing that made our family acceptable to the Tiptons was our money.'

'That's true, isn't it?'

Bertram broke off a piece of toast and inspected it. 'Yes, but you don't expect a fellow to say so. Especially not when he's marrying one's sister.'

He put the toast down and reached for the marmalade. 'I don't know if you've noticed, but Tipton's been getting more and more above himself.'

'I met – well heard – his mother last night. She's awful.'

'Yes, I heard Amelia never liked him much, but she'll enjoy the wedding.'

'What about his father?'

'Turning up only for the wedding by all accounts. Maybe he'll be able to keep him in check. From what I remember Tipton was always terrified of him.'

I sipped some of the strong, hot, black coffee. It was excellent. 'It's not exactly a case of a happy wedding, is it?'

'I don't know,' said Bertram finally crunching into his toast and spitting crumbs across the tablecloth. 'I think Tippy and Richenda are getting pretty much what they want.'

'Your table manners are terrible,' I said. Bertram had the grace to blush. 'I suppose I should be minding my Ps and Qs more with you seeing as you're, you know.' He jerked his head meaningfully to one side.

'My mother always said that regardless of his company a true gentleman always displays a gentleman's manners.'

'Your mother?' said Bertram. 'You've not told me much about her. Who was she before she married the vicar? Someone with pretentions I presume. Your manners have been impeccable, so far. You seem far more at home here than any of us Staplefords. You even managed to keep that other old codger amused last night and he's notoriously snobby.'

'Really,' I said trying to change the subject, 'I found him very gossipy.'

'You're changing the subject,' said Bertram. 'This toast is burnt.'

'The food last night was terrible.'

Bertram rolled his eyes. 'I had to get Rory to make me up a digestion remedy.'

'How is he faring as your valet?'

'Tolerably,' said Bertram. 'He's a smart one. Never needs to be told anything twice. Richard hasn't thrown anything at him yet, so he must find him suitable too. Makes a better butler though. I don't think he has enough to do here. He's being very broody. Taciturn for the most part, but alarmingly Scotch when he does speak. He's definitely missing Stapleford Hall.'

'Only three more days to go and this will all be over.'

'Yes, thank goodness,' said Bertram.

We both fell silent. I thought how very easy it had been to talk to Bertram as an equal. We were almost like some old married couple over break-fast. We spoke with the ease of long intimacy. I wondered what he would do when I told him Rory and I were to be wed. He'd certainly never talk to me like this again. We would be sundered by class more completely than ever before. My chest felt heavy. I needed to ask one of the maids for an indigestion remedy myself.

I finished my coffee and stood up. I was about to make my polite adieu's when the double doors of the dining room flew open. Hanging between them, a hand on each handle, was Merry. She opened her mouth and screamed. Bertram dropped his coffee cup. The black stain spread out across the white linen. Merry screamed again.

Chapter Fifteen

A Murder is Announced

Robbins threw a jug of water over Merry. She stopped screaming and slapped him. Then she screamed again. Robbins staggered backwards. Bertram was on his feet, dithering. I ran over to the sodden Merry and took her firmly by the shoulders. I gave her a little shake. 'What has happened?'

'She's dead,' said my friend. 'She's dead.'

My heart sunk down to my feet. 'Who is dead, Merry?'

'Lady Stapleford.'

I brought Merry over to the table. 'Robbins, fetch this girl a brandy. She has had a bad shock.' I caught sight of Bertram slumping back down in his seat. 'And another for Mr Bertram.'

104

'Right away, ma'am,' said Robbins, only too keen to be given something to do far away from the hysterical Merry.

Drips from Merry's hair trickled across her face and mixed with her tears. 'Oh, Euphemia,' she said, 'it's dreadful. I crept in to see if she needed me yet and she was just lying there.'

'Stabbed?' I asked.

'N-no.'

'Strangled?'

'N-no.'

'Then what?'

'Just lying there.'

'She was sleeping, you stupid girl,' snapped Bertram.

'I think I knows the difference between a sleeping body and a dead one,' growled Merry. Then, adding as an afterthought, 'sir.'

'Is there any chance you could be mistaken?' I asked gently.

'Oh no, Euphemia, there was vomit everywhere.'

'Poisoned, then,' I said.

'Oh my God,' said Bertram and put his head in his hands. 'My poor mother. That awful food last night must have been too much for her. Oh, Mama!'

'I think I should go up and check,' I said resolutely. The thought of entering a vomit-covered room was not enticing.

Robbins returned with the brandies. 'I will fetch Mrs Merion,' he said. 'I'm sure the young lady is mistaken. I would rather not notify the Earl until we are absolutely sure.'

Merry opened her mouth to protest. I shoved the brandy glass into her hand and gave her a quelling look. 'An excellent idea, Robbins,' I said.

Within a very short space of time he returned bringing with him a bustling Mrs Merion and, to my great surprise, Rory. 'I'm sorry, ma'am,' she said, 'but when he overheard what had happened he insisted on coming. I thought it might be a good idea to have a man present.'

I nodded and tried not to betray the great relief I felt at seeing Rory.

The three of us made our way quickly to the upper floor and along to Lady Stapleford's room. Outside, we all three hesitated. I took a deep breath and knocked loudly. Silence. I knocked again. Richenda's door opened. 'What the devil are you doing making such a racket at this time in the morning?'

'If you could please do back into your room, miss,' said Mrs Merion.

'Rory? What is going on? Why are you standing outside my stepmama's room?'

'We fear she may have been taken ill,' replied Rory.

'Then what are you all doing standing out here?' demanded Richenda. She strode across the corridor and flung open the door. An intensive smell of vomit wafted over us. It was only with difficulty that I kept my scrambled eggs in place. Richenda staggered back. Rory and I, as one, went forward.

Lady Stapleford lay curled on her side. The bedclothes were disarrayed as if she had been thrashing about. There was vomit on the sheets, her nightgown and even on the floor. But worse than that as Rory flung back the curtain to let in the light, I saw her face sheet white and set in an expression of agony.

Rory opened a window, leant out and was sick himself. To be absolutely sure I went up to Lady Stapleford and touched her lightly on the forehead. She was ice-cold and most definitely dead.

As I stepped away my foot trod on something and I almost fell. It was a half a tea-cup, quite empty but smashed on the ground beside its saucer. When Rory drew his head back into the room, I pointed silently at it. Our eyes met and I knew he understood the seriousness of the situation.

'Come on, Mrs Merion,' he said. 'We must lock this room.'

'Whatever for?' cried the housekeeper. 'We must arrange matters for this poor lady. We cannot have her nearest and dearest seeing her like this!'

Rory put his hands on her shoulders and gently hustled her out of the room. 'We must call the police,' he said. 'We need to tell them there's been a murder.'

Chapter Sixteen

The Incredulity of the Aristocracy

Mrs Merion didn't part easily with her key, but Rory managed to get the room locked. She scuttled off at once, clutching her chatelaine as if she feared we would seize more keys.

'You saw the cup,' I said to Rory.

'She might hae knocked it o'er when she was – yer ken–'

'Dying?' I suggested.

'Aye,' said Rory looking at his feet. 'Yer should nae be talking to me.'

'I think in times of crisis the barriers between the classes can be ignored,' I said.

'Then yer donnae ken what yer talking aboot, lassie.'

I shook my head dismissively. 'I expect she has gone to inform the Earl. We should follow.'

Rory gave me an unfathomable look, 'Do yer no think someone should be telling Mr Bertram that his mother is definitely dead?'

'Ah, yes, Bertram,' I said. Rory winced as I used his Christian name. 'Yes, you go after Mrs Merion and I'll go and check on Bertram.'

'Yes ma'am,' said Rory. He walked away quickly.

I stood for a minute in front of the bedroom door thinking about what lay behind it. Murder was an occupational habit of being a Stapleford as far as I could tell and I have no doubts that something unpleasant, even evil, was afoot. I had disliked Lady Stapleford, but she was a mother. Bertram had lost his mother and I knew what it was like to lose a parent. I would respect the dead lady for her son's sake. I silently said a short prayer I had heard my father say so many times over the recently deceased. Then I went to find Bertram.

I found him still at the breakfast table. It did not surprise me that he had not chosen to follow us. An impulsive man at heart, Bertram was constitutionally opposed to believing how very dark things could be. He had to be. He lived in the same house as a brother who he believed had murdered their father. In short he was always reluctant to face and deal with unpleasant truths.

He rose as I entered the room. 'Euphemia, is Mama well?' I came forward and took his hands in mind. 'I am so sorry, Bertram, but your mother is dead.'

At this precise moment Rory walked into the room and saw my hands in Bertram's. A scowl descended on his face, but he replaced it quickly with an appropriate sombre look. I had not missed the flash of jealousy in his eyes. All I could think was, not now. Honestly men.

Bertram gave a short cry, released my hands and sank back down into his seat. Richard Stapleford moved behind his chair and placed his hand on Bertram's shoulder forcing me to cede my place.

I realised the room had become a lot fuller of people than when I had left. 'Bear up, Bertie, old man,' said Richard. He swallowed hard. 'We both know what it's like to lose a parent.' He squeezed Bertram's shoulder firmly. 'It'll be fine, old man. You, Rory, fetch this man another brandy.' I simmered with fury. I knew how false this man was being, but Bertram looked up at him with real gratitude in his eyes. He nodded, obviously blinking back tears. 'It's the shock,' he said to Richard. 'She was so young.'

The phrase *not as young as she would like people to think* flashed through my mind. 'We have to think of what she want,' said Richard. 'Should we postpone the wedding?'

'Oh no,' said Bertram, 'Mama would not want that. She was so looking forward to it.' He choked on the last words. Rory silently handed him a glass. 'I think I'd like to be alone for a bit,' said Bertram. 'If someone could call a doctor? I'll make the arrangements once her death has been medically confirmed.'

'Of course, Bertie. Of course. You go up for a bit,' said Richard.

'Excuse me,' I said, 'but I don't think you will find it is that straightforward.'

'What?' said Bertram.

'I am very much afraid that Lady Stapleford has been murdered.' A ripple of interest went round the room.

'You dare,' gasped Bertram, 'you dare say that! Who do you suggest wanted my mother dead?'

I took a step backwards. 'I have no idea,' I said.

'Exactly,' said Bertram, 'there is no one who would have wanted to harm my mother. I'll thank you to keep your fantasies to yourself.' He stormed

110

off, still clutching the glass. Richard raised an eyebrow at me.

'You'll have to excuse the fellow, Your Highness,' said the Earl's voice from behind me. 'The fellow's a bit upset.'

'Of course,' I said, turning to face Ratty. 'But as I am sure your housekeeper and the Stapleford's valet would have told you, it appears Lady Stapleford drunk her late night drink before she died.'

'Nothing odd in that,' said the Earl. 'Did the same thing myself.'

'Yes, but you appear to be quite hale.'

'Oh, you're saying someone deliberately put something in her drink?' said the Earl, frowned in a very craggy way. 'I thought young Bertram had picked you up wrong and you meant she'd died of food poisoning.'

Mrs Merion tugged at his sleeve. 'I did say I was concerned about the oyster supplier.'

The Countess came up beside her husband. 'Perhaps we should send the servants to check that no one else is feeling unwell?' she suggested.

'An excellent idea,' I said in what I hoped was a compromising tone. 'But the doctor must also be sent for.'

'What, young Leech?' said the Earl. 'He's the only man in these parts and he's barely out of nappies.'

The Countess patted his arm. 'Threep. He's a fully qualified young man and I'm sure he'd be delighted to help. Now someone will have to go and tell Richenda. I believe she is still in bed. Regardless of what Bertram said, I am not at all sure it is proper for the wedding to continue.'

'Lady Stapleford's maid should also be found,' I said as I had a sudden vision of Suzette running away with what remained of Lady Stapleford' s jewellery.

'Indeed,' said the Countess. 'An excellent idea. She may well be able to clear up all this confusion. You, girl, put that glass down and go and find her. Send her to Mrs Merion's room.'

A white-faced Merry, stood shakily, bobbed a curtsey and left.

'Now you, my dear, as Richenda's closest friend, are undoubtedly the right person to break the news to her and ascertain what she wishes to do.' I turned and looked hopefully over my shoulder, but she was talking to me.

Chapter Seventeen

The Blushing Bride

'The witch,' cried Richenda, 'She has done this to spite me!'

'She died in agony,' I said. We were standing in Richenda's room. The lady was clad in an unflattering olive bed jacket and matching nightdress. It certainly didn't sit well with the puce colour suffusing her face.

It had not gone unnoticed that while I had a suite of rooms, she only had an overly large room. Strange red birds, shedding feathers and golden pagodas adorned the wallpaper. Little blue farmers with baskets and triangular hats were frozen in their attempt to cross little bridges that led from one tree to another. Indisputably exotic, the patterned papers and accompanying linen and curtains were very busy. It was giving me a headache. I thought if I'd been cooped up in here for a night I might be in a foul mood too.

'Over-ate, did she?' said Richenda, stamping her foot. 'Greedy cow. Always was out for whatever she could get for free. I'll tell you one thing I will not let her indispositions halt my wedding.'

'Indisposition?' I said, 'the lady is dead.'

Richenda waved her hand dismissively. 'Don't worry. I shall say how awfully sorry I am and all that and how dear Stepmama wanted this wedding so very much. I shall dedicate the wedding to her memory. Even if the words stick in my throat. I'll tell you, Euphemia, that woman got no more than she deserved.'

Merry, who was searching for black clothes for Richenda to wear or anything even vaguely suitable for mourning, poked her head out from the cupboard. 'I always thought she was alright,' she said stubbornly. 'She was the only one who ever spoke up to your father for you.'

'Merry!' I hissed. 'It is not your place to say such things.'

'It's true,' said Merry. 'And I don't hold with speaking ill of the dead. Lady Stapleford didn't do me no wrong and I'm sorry she's copped it.'

'Perhaps we should have you read the eulogy at the funeral?' said Richenda, dripping sarcasm.

Merry came completely out of the wardrobe, so she could stand her ground. 'All I'm saying is she didn't deserve to be murdered.' She sniffed and muttered under the breath, 'unlike some I could mention.'

But she needn't have worried Richenda had already turned her fury on me. 'This is your fault.'

'Me?' I staggered backwards. 'I didn't kill her.'

'Of course not. She ate too many oysters or some such, but I have no doubt it will have been you who cried murder. Still trying to get your claws into Bertram. He'll never have you.'

'Might I suggest,' I said reverting to my own upper-class accent (and I can make it as painful as long nails running across wet china) 'that it would be incredibly foolish of me to attract the police's attention to The Court. I am not, after all, who I am thought to be.' I added a mental if you only you knew.

'Pah!' said Richenda.

'I could further add that any investigation that unmasks me will also unmask the person who presented me to the company. You, Richenda, you!'

'Blast it,' said Richenda and threw herself down on the bed. 'What's the Earl doing about it?'

'He has sent for the local doctor.'

'Old family doctor?' I could hear the hope in her voice. I shook my head. 'No, apparently a new man. Young and freshly qualified.'

'Well, you will just have to wrap him round your finger, Euphemia, like you seem to do with all the men you meet. You've got a head start this time. You're royalty.'

'Are you suggesting that I ask the doctor to falsify his account?'

'I'm saying if it is murder then yes, you need to

114

get him under control. I'm sure the Earl can see off any policemen. It'll all be over by tomorrow.'

She stalked over to the wardrobe, pushed Merry aside and pulled out a dark blue dress. 'This will do. It's not like she was blood.'

I left and Merry took the opportunity to come with me under the pretence of helping me change into something less dressy than the beautiful red frock I was wearing. 'She's going to get us all into trouble if she carries on like that,' said Merry and she helped me with the impossible fastenings. 'Are you sure it was murder?'

'I don't know. Rory thought the same as me. It was the empty cup. No sign of a stain on the floor from that. It was obviously the last thing she'd drunk.'

'How are you going to work this one out?' asked Merry. 'I'll help as much as I can, but I'm stuck below stairs most of the time. And Rory can hardly come up and gossip with you.'

'No,' I said sadly, 'and Bertram is furious with me for suggesting someone had murdered his mother.'

'He'll get over that once he realises you're right.'

'I hope so. If it is murder then the murderer has to be found quickly before the police ask too many questions.'

'You don't suppose Richenda did it after that awful row they had last night?'

I thought about it. 'It depends what the row was about. Richenda wouldn't do anything to put her grand day in danger.'

'But if that was what Lady Stapleford was threatening to do?' said Merry.

'I can see how she might think that was the lesser of two evils. After all, she has seen her brother get away with murder.'

'So you say.'

'If you are about to say, Merry, that it was never proved. Then I know that.'

Merry huffed. 'I suppose if you're used to getting your own way in everything you might take it a step too far. Richard saw off the police before...' she trailed off. 'I hope the Earl is the same or you're in a lot of trouble.'

I stopped stung with indignation. 'Are you saying you want the murderer to go Scot-free to save us a little inconvenience?'

'If by inconvenience you mean jail then yes, I'm leaning that way. I'm in on it too and more to the point so are all the Staplefords. There is no way they are going to let the police swarm over this household.'

I lifted my head resolutely. 'Then it will be up to us to catch him – or her,' I said.

'Oh Lor',' said Merry. 'You and your grand ideas.'

'Where's the Merry I once knew, who would have said what a grand adventure?'

'Did you bang your head?' said Merry. 'I've never thought anything you've got yourself into was a grand adventure. I should have left you locked in that wardrobe.' And so saying she took herself off into one of the servants' passageways still muttering. I reflected that Merry with a serious swain was a lot less fun. It was clear she wanted to keep her head down and get permission to marry Merrit. I could hear her now explaining

116

to Richenda how they were so well-suited, both liking 'views'.

I entered the morning room. There was probably more than one morning room in this vast pile, but it was the only one I had been shown. My grandfather and the Earl were seated by the fireside sipping whisky. Both rose as I entered.

'I'm so sorry,' I said preparing to back out. 'I didn't mean to disturb you.'

The Earl came over and held out his hand. 'Do come in my dear girl. We could do with some beauty to lighten the mood.'

My grandfather sheepishly pushed his glass to one side. 'I know it's a bit early, but we've all had a bit of a shock. We both knew Lady Stapleford in her youth before she married the late Lord Stapleford. Believe it or not, she was once rather a lovely girl.'

I could see no way to politely make my escape, so I took a chair on the opposite side of the fire and refused 'a snifter' from the Earl. 'Ah, such a long time since we were all young,' said Ratty (the Earl's nickname.) 'You wouldn't understand Lily dear, but I'm afraid you will one day. Age comes to us all.'

'If we're lucky,' muttered my grandfather.

'Quite. Quite.' said Ratty.

'Yes, quite a beauty, she was,' said my grandfather, 'I remember my late wife was most unkind about her.'

Ratty smiled. It was always a good test of a girl's looks if Charlotte disliked her. His,' he gestured to my grandfather, 'wife was one of the most beautiful women you could ever have wished to meet.'

My grandfather nodded sadly. 'She took it badly when her looks began to fade.'

Ratty swallowed a good mouthful of whisky. 'They often do. I've been lucky with the Countess. She never was that much of a looker, but brains, wit, and charm, they never fade, and she has them all in abundance.'

'Bowled over, I was,' said my grandfather, 'I thought such a heavenly creature must have the temperament of an angel. Couldn't believe my luck when she said yes.'

Ratty hiccupped slightly. 'We're still talking about your late wife, aren't we?'

Grandfather assented. 'I'd have done anything for that woman. And I did. Made some foolish promises.' His face creased in sorrow. 'Word of a gentleman and all that. Never should have done it.'

Ratty got up rather unsteadily and placed a hand on his shoulder. I was becoming uncomfortably aware that they had dipped into the decanter rather more than I had realised. It wasn't even eleven o'clock.

'What will happen about the wedding?' I asked.

'I doubt the Stapleford girl will let Tipton slip through her fingers. She'll have a quiet do. Doubtless say it was what her stepmama would have wanted. No one will believe her, but it'll pass muster.'

'Wasn't there to be a wedding rehearsal this morning?' I asked.

'Damn and blast it,' said the Earl. He went to the fireplace and vigorously rang the bell. 'Someone will have to tell the vicar he's on double time!'

Chapter Eighteen

Is There a Doctor in the House?

'She's in here, doctor,' said Rory unlocking Lady Stapleford's door.

'I can't face it,' cried Richenda. 'Poor Step-mama!' She swooned dramatically. No one caught her. She hit the floor with a dull thud.

Dr Threep, a man in his early thirties dressed in poor quality tweeds, and with glasses constantly sliding down his nose, gave a little 'Eep!'

'Is she alright?' he asked.

'Oh, aye,' said Rory, 'but she was that close to her wed...' he coughed. 'I mean that close to her stepmama. It's affected her. Perhaps you'd be able to give her a sedative, doctor?'

'No, I'm fi–', began Richenda, struggling to her feet, but the Countess secured her by the arm. 'I think that's an excellent idea,' she said. 'I'll see Richenda along to her room and you can see her afterwards, doctor. Her Highness can represent the household. My husband really can't stand bodily fluids. The trouble I had getting pregnant you would not believe! And Robbins is a bit old for such things.'

And with that she left Rory and I with the doctor. 'Is this the way the house normally runs?' he asked Rory.

'I'm afraid I couldn't say, sir. Neither her

119

Fingal County Libraries

Highness nor I are of this household.'

'Then why? No, never mind. I think I'll stick to the job at hand. You are aware, your Highness, that this is liable to be unpleasant.'

'It was Rory, the housekeeper and I who discovered the body.'

'Well, I only hope she kept the windows shut,' said the doctor obscurely and flung the door wide. He stepped through. This time the stench was stronger. The natural procedure of dying had added other elements to the mess that doubtless Ratty would have found most uncomfortable. The window was open and flies were buzzing around... I felt the gorge rise in my throat. I took a step back into the corridor. Rory looked at me anxiously.

'You're gey white,' he said under his breath.

'It's all right,' I said. 'I'm not going in.'

'My, my!' said the doctor from within. 'Not a pretty sight at all. I can definitely say she ate something that disagreed with her with monumental consequences.' He sounded positively gleeful. 'I'd need to perform an autopsy to be sure, but I think we can put it down to food poisoning.' He came back to the doorway. 'Any chance the family would let me do an autopsy?' he asked.

'Absolutely not,' shouted Richard Stapleford, striding down the corridor. 'Why was I not informed the doctor was here?' he demanded.

'I have no idea,' I said coldly.

'Well, I am here now and there can be no question of cutting up dear Mama.'

'Isn't that your brother's decision,' I asked. 'As it is actually his mother and not yours?'

'Good God, woman – I mean, your Highness! I

120

don't know how things are down in your country, but here we respect the dead.'

'Just thought I'd ask,' said the doctor. 'Usually only get to practice my cutting skills on the odd sheep or pig one of the local farmers is feeling a bit iffy about.'

His mournful expression at the loss of Lady Stapleford's cadaver in other circumstances would have been almost comical. I attempted to see past the general despicableness of the little man and focus attention on the real matter. 'Did you notice the cup, doctor?'

'Er,' the medic blinked at me. 'Pretty floral thing on its side with a smashed saucer?'

'Yes, exactly. Did you happen to notice if it was full or empty?'

The doctor scratched his head and some of his scalp came away with his fingernails. He picked it out thoughtfully. 'Empty, yes.'

'And was there a corresponding stain on the carpet?' I asked.

'Just a mo,' he said and ducked back into the room. Coming back out, 'I see what you mean. Have the police been called?' Obviously, apart from his unsavoury penchant for dead flesh, he knew mysterious circumstances when he saw them. He went up a notch in my estimation. Which still kept him at well below zero.

'This is an Earl's seat,' thundered Richard, 'we can't have grubby-faced constables running riot though it. It's not done.'

The doctor slid his glasses once more up his nose. 'Why don't we go and ask the Earl?' he said. Rory locked the door and dropped the key

121

in his pocket.

Ratty found himself confronted in the morning room by four people who all wanted something quite different from him. Richard blustered. The doctor warned him. I wanted the thing handled properly and Rory wanted permission to head back below stairs. Despite his early morning snifters with my grandfather I observed the Earl's gaze kept slipping longingly towards the decanter, now back in its tantalus. The Earl drew his face into its craggiest wrinkles and said, 'Where's my wife?'

Rory leapt at this opportunity to get away from the limelight and went in search of the Countess. 'I think you should come with me, doctor,' he said. 'You were going to give Miss Richenda a wee drop of something to calm her down.'

'Oh yes. Yes, indeed,' said Threep. 'Don't worry, Earl. I'll be back in a moment.'

When the door had shut behind them the Earl sat down. 'Pour us all a drink, will you Richard? Now the riff-raff's gone we can discuss this thing properly.'

Knowing when he was outgunned, Richard did as he was bid, even going as far as to pour me a very, very, very small Scotch. Fortunately I have no liking for Scotch – the liquid kind at least. We all sat down around the fire. 'Hopefully,' said Ratty, 'me wife will come back and tell us a few of the others had a gippy tummy last night, and then we can put it down to an acute sensitivity and unfortunate accident for Lady Stapleford.'

'Glad to hear that, sir,' said Richard.

Ratty frowned even harder. 'I don't mind admitting the food last night was particularly poor. Cook must have been out of sorts about something. But if we end up blaming the poor lady's demise on her cooking I can tell you this household is in for a devil of time. Do you know how hard it is to get decent staff?'

'Very hard,' I chipped in. 'And we certainly wouldn't want the woman to carry a death on her conscience if in fact it was nothing to do with her.'

The Earl looked at me as if I was a pot plant that had just spoken. 'Er, yes, my dear, quite.'

'I don't care about some servant's blasted feelings, saving your presence, sir. I do care very much about some country doctor mauling about the body of my dead stepmother. By Gad, it's not to be thought of.'

The Earl looked him steadily in the eye. 'But you must see, my good fellow, that losing a cook is a very serious business.' Richard shot to his feet and opened his mouth, but what blistering retort he had in mind we never heard as at this moment the Countess entered the room with Rory and the doctor following behind like ducklings with their mother. She came over and placed a hand on her husband's shoulder. 'No, dear, you mustn't upset yourself, it's not good for your heart.' Rory and the doctor followed her into the room. The Countess turned a surprisingly stony countenance towards us all. 'I have spoken with Mrs Merion, Cook and all the relevant servants. I can confirm there were a few mild cases of indigestion due to Cook falling below par last night. She had heard her nephew Tommy is up for poaching again.' She patted the Earl's shoulder. 'I told her that you would sort it all out. Thank goodness the under-cook was on hand to deliver breakfast! Good enough girl in her way, but not a patch on Cook when she's running to form. Should have her up and trotting for lunch today!'

'That's a relief,' said the Earl.

'I have also,' continued the Countess, 'spoken to Mrs Merion. She had some fears over our oyster suppliers. I can assume these were unfounded as no one else suffered any symptoms similar to the late Lady Stapleford.'

'An allergy,' said Richard Stapleford.

'The cadaver does not present with signs that would suggest that was the cause of death,' said Threep. Richard gave him a filthy look, but the doctor stood his ground and pushed his spectacles back up his nose with an almost defiant air.

'Sadly, my dear, I fear we must inform the police we have an unexplained death. Isn't Ronnie something to do with a police board or some such thing. Perhaps he could get us an amiable, cleverish sort of chap, who could tie this all up quickly?'

'Is that really necessary,' said Ratty. 'We're not really the sort that answer to, er – to that sort, are we?'

'The problem,' said Countess forestalling another outburst from Richard, 'is that we have Royalty present. Foreign Royalty.' There was a weighty pause. Now was the time for Richard or I to disclose our deception. Our eyes met. I saw a challenge in his. If I gave myself up I would not be able to count on his support. I lowered my eyes, ashamed of myself. The Countess continued to speak. 'This could be blown up into quite a diplomatic incident if we're not careful. I've ordered the house gates to be closed, but we cannot trust the lower staff not to gossip or worse still attempt to sell the story to a,' she swallowed and pronounced the next word with obvious distaste, 'a newspaper man.'

'Oh, by Gad, no!' said the Earl. 'This family has never had a scandal and we're not having one now!'

The Countess raised an eyebrow.

'You know what I mean,' he said. 'We've never had outsiders involved in our business.'

'That's why I suggest we get someone calm and discreet to tie this all up.'

'Yes, I see,' said Ratty. 'Brainy one, my wife.'

'And the body?' said Threep. His nose positively twitched with excitement making his glasses do a funny sort of jig.

'I have had it removed to one of our cold stores. I've called for someone from the village to lay her out formally.'

'But the police need to see the body at the scene of the crime,' I said.

The Countess turned flinty eyes on me. 'Those were some of my very best sheets. They are being boiled at this minute.' She took a breath. 'Not that I would want to appear obstructive. I will order that Lady Stapleford's clothes are preserved in their current state and that apart from the bed the room will be left as it was found. If there is any further evidence I assume it will mainly be in the body of the deceased. Am I right, doctor?'

'Oh yes.' said Threep. 'I've the perfect facilities.'

Richard roared in fury.

'Stop that at once, young man. You will behave as a gentleman in the presence of ladies,' said the Countess. Richard reddened. 'I personally would prefer that Lady Stapleford had a quick and decent burial and we could all move on to a happier event. Hopefully my husband will be able to find a policeman who thinks in the same way.'

'Thank you,' said Richard. 'I shall inform her son.'

'I expect he would like to see her. The village women are quite adapt in the way of things and I should imagine he could safely say his farewells in around an hour without being unduly disturbed by her appearance.'

'Is there anything I can do to help?' I said.

The Countess looked shocked. 'My dear, you are royalty. You should have nothing to do with this or anything else. Perhaps if you could all retire to your rooms and attempt to persuade any of the other guests to do the same. We could all spend a little time in reflection on the ephemeral nature of life. Hopefully by the time luncheon is served the police will have come and gone.'

So it was to be a white-wash. Rory opened the door for me. I could see he wasn't happy about any of this either, but I could hardly discuss the matter with him. As I left the room I heard a snatch of whispered conversation between the Earl and his wife. 'These young people. They don't understand the importance of keeping a decent cook,' said Ratty. 'Or of decent linen,' said the Countess with deep distain.

Chapter Nineteen

Waiting for the Police

I returned to my room as I had been requested only to find Merry waiting for me. 'So! So!' she cried as I entered the room, bouncing up from her chair like an excitable puppy. 'What's going to happen?' I told her the full extent of the conversation in the morning room.

'A white-wash,' said Merry, unknowingly echoing my own thoughts.

'He could be a decent policeman,' I said.

'Please,' said Merry, 'there is two Earls present and one Countess, not to mention Your Highness's royal self. There is no way he'd want to make trouble.'

'Then we need to present him with uncontroversial proof,' I said stoutly.

'What you need is to watch your back,' said Merry. 'Ain't it occurred to you that if the police find out who you really are then you'll be in a heap of trouble. The Staplefords won't back you up. They will say they were hoodwinked too.'

'But it wouldn't add up!'

Merry screwed up her face.

'Merry! Are you feeling quite well?'

''Ang on, I'm thinking.' The scowl faded. 'Yep, reckon you're right it wouldn't add up. The only thing they could do to be sure would be to off you too.'

'What? Then my identity would definitely come out!'

Merry nodded slowly. 'True. But what if they made look as if you had killed yourself? Made it out you were so afraid of being caught out that...'

'Merry, what on earth is giving you such ideas?'

'See when you're in your bed late tonight. You think about my words and see if they don't make sense then.'

'Who do you think did it?' I asked trying to turn Merry's mind to less ghoulish fantasies.

'Richenda, Richard, Tipton or Bertram.'

'Bertram!' I said astounded.

'Before I met you I didn't know nothing about murdering, but if there's anything these past two years have shown me, it's that you never can tell who will do what and why.'

'It would have to be someone who knew her, wouldn't it?' I said. 'Both the Earls, the Countess and Renard Layfette knew her. In fact she hated Renard Layfette and wouldn't even allow his name to be mentioned in her presence. There's a history there.'

'And 'ow are you going to find about it?'

'I'm going to ask him.'

Merry sighed. 'I guess I'm going to have to watch out for you, aren't I? Seeing as how you're set on getting yourself into a whole heap of trouble. I don't know what my Merrit's going to say about it all. I really don't.'

'Could you find out who delivered the late night drink to her room? The little maid who makes my fire in the morning, Daisy, said it was a Lucy who's meant to do the drinks, but she's a bit shy and can leave them outside the room instead of knocking.'

'Which would give someone the perfect opportunity to drop something in it,' said Merry thoughtfully. 'I've seen Daisy. Strikes me she could be a right little chatterbox if you let her.'

I nodded. 'Right. I'll start with her. But it does beg a question. Did someone intend to poison Lady Stapleford right the way along, so they had the poison on hand or was it a spur of the moment thing?'

'The only way we'll know that,' I said, 'is when or if we find out what poisoned her.'

Merry nodded. 'Yeah, any big house like this is a poisoner's delight from rat poison to the stuff they clean the silver with – and that's not mentioning any of the stuff the gardeners use.'

'So once we know what it is ... I'll have to make that doctor tell me... We'll be able to work out who had the opportunity to get the poison.'

'Right then, you set to charming the police and that doctor and I'll start with a little chat with our Daisy.'

When Merry had gone I sat down to think. I couldn't very well ignore the Countess's request that we spent the time between now and luncheon thinking about the deceased. I thought mainly of how I would like to write my thoughts down, so I could untangle the warring ideas in my head. However, although I intended to do this later at my leisure the chances of an inquisitive maid coming across my notes was too great a risk. But then again not all maids could read. Daisy would probably use it for kindling. I turned things round and round in my head. It simply didn't make sense that the Staplefords were involved in this. As far as I knew Lady Stapleford had been all for the wedding. I believed she had intended to use the opportunity to launch herself back into society and find herself a new husband. Heavens, my grandfather could even have been one of her targets. This did not bear thinking about. The luncheon bell sounded. (A gong for dinner. A bell for luncheon. I wondered if this was to ensure guests who spent all their time inebriated would be able to tell which was which.)

I headed downstairs only to be informed by Robbins that luncheon had been laid out buffet style in the garden room. 'The doors are open onto the terrace, your Highness,' he said. 'I believe you will not find the prospect unpleasing.' I thanked him politely, mentally noting yet again that it was the staff who not only behaved better, but often spoke better than their supposed 'betters'.

Silver cutlery flashed and crystal twinkled on the well-laden table. Before me lay a feast that even Mrs Deighton would have found hard to beat. My stomach growled in a most unladylike manner at the sight of real food after last night's debacle. I picked up a plate and began to happily serve myself. Other guests milled around me, but for the first few minutes the glorious food held my attention. Quails eggs! Buttered lobster! Asparagus spears in a hollandaise sauce, so light and creamy it positively caressed my tongue. Delighted with my spoils, I tucked in with gusto. I was sucking the meat from a heavenly lobster tail when I became aware someone had sat down beside me.

'You are very brave,' said Renard Layfette's voice, 'or is it merely what the English call "having phlegm"?'

I took the lobster from between my lips. It made a most unfortunate sound. 'What do you mean?' I asked, trying to brazen my blushes out.

'Why, that someone has died of poisoning in this house after eating the food.'

I looked down at my half-consumed plate and felt suddenly less hungry. 'What did you think I meant?' continued Layfette. 'Is there another secret that you are keeping?'

'I understand you and Lady Stapleford were at odds,' I challenged in an attempt to distract him.

Renard gave a Gallic shrug. 'Me, I say live and let live. Lady Stapleford held other views.'

'What do you mean?'

'She disapproved of my lifestyle.'

I waited for him to say more. This was a man who loved attention and the sound of his own voice.

'It is an old story. I was a little wild in my youth. All the most interesting people are, I find, don't you? But you are still young. Maybe there is time yet left for you to be – interesting.'

I could not think of an answer to this, so I remained silent. However, I did feel insulted. Layfette gave a little laugh. 'Forgive. I am surprised to find it still rankles. My father disowned me. He is, of course, dead now. Whole swathes of society set their face against me. Yet here I am, so many years later, dining at the table of an Earl. In the end I am the survivor, the winner.'

'And how did Lady Stapleford feel about your presence here?'

'I have no idea. I did not talk to her. I expect she was not happy. But what could she say? Her husband is dead and she is poor now and of no account.'

'Especially because she is dead,' I pointed out.

'Tant pis!' said Renard. 'Life must go on. I shall leave you to enjoy your lobster in peace.'

All at once I felt very vulnerable and out of my depth. I left my plate half-finished, declined anything sweet and left the room. Conversation buzzed behind me, but I told myself continuing to ask questions in a crowded room would only draw attention. As I wandered into the hallway I made a discovery. I had nothing to do. Without the consolidating focus of the wedding rehearsals all the guests were left high and dry. Some of the men might retire to smoke, drink whisky and play cards, but for the ladies there was only tea and cake – and we had only just had luncheon. If I had been at home at Stapleford Hall – how strange to think of it as home – I would be overloaded with tasks. I missed being busy. I could not imagine how the Earl and his cronies made their way so aimlessly through life. A life my mother had always wanted for me, but I was now quite certain I would never want for myself.

A tap on my shoulder made me jump. Lord Milford, also known as Fitzroy, stood beside me. 'If I could ask Your Highness to accompany me to the small library for a moment?' he asked with extreme politeness.

I felt a weight lift from my shoulders. Of course, here was the very man to sort out all this nastiness. I gave him what I hoped was a stunning smile and nodded.

The small library was in a corner turret room and was indeed deficient in space. However, it had large windows that gave out over the wild flower garden and fountain. I imagined many an Earl or Viscount had whiled away hours in here 'reading' while staring out of the window at the heavenly view.

'I am so glad to see you,' I said as Fitzroy closed the door.

'How very flattering,' he said. He came across to the table and opened a small folder. 'I hope you are not foolish enough to think I will let myself get embroiled in this fiasco?'

'Fiasco! The woman was murdered?'

'Was she?' asked Fitzroy levelly. 'I don't believe there has been anything more than conjecture at present. Your conjecture. Personally, when working under an alias I consider it wise to remain as inconspicuous as possible.'

'You mean you would let justice fail because you don't want people to know you are not Lord Milford?'

'Who says I am not? This may be my real name.'

'Is it?'

'Some time ago you and Mr MacLeod were kind enough to sign some papers to keep ensure you kept the matter that occurred in the Highlands secret.'

'This is why you wanted to see me?'

'Euphemia, rid yourself of the idea that I have

an interest in Lady Stapleford's death.' He put up a hand to stop me from retorting. 'Even if she was murdered, I simply do not care to draw attention to myself, nor do I have any interest in catching a domestic murderer should there actually be one!'

'But Richard Stapleford is involved! You said you wanted to hear of anything unusual that occurred with the family.'

'I believe that was Mr Edward rather than myself. Now, here I have a copy of what is to be known as the official secrets act. I'd be grateful if you could sign it now.'

'And if I don't?'

Fitzroy raised an eyebrow. 'Do not imagine for one moment that you can blackmail me into helping you solve this mystery.'

I jumped on this. 'So you agree there is a mystery!'

Fitzroy held out a pen to me. 'Sign.' I hesitated. 'You know how efficient I can be. I need all the loose ends of the Highland incident tidied.' He paused. 'One way or another.'

In spite of the heat from the sunlight pouring through the glass I found myself shivering.

'Exactly. Now be a good girl.'

I very much wished I could slap him, but regardless of what title or name he used I knew Fitzroy was no gentleman and would have no qualms about slapping me back or worse. I put my chin up. 'For King and country,' I said and signed.

'Well played,' said the hateful Fitzroy. 'Knowing when to yield the field is a most important skill. If not *the* most important skill.'

'If you think I am going to give up trying to find the murderer of Lady Stapleford you are quite mistaken.'

'The police have been called, Euphemia.'

'And we both know how much influence the regular police have in high society, don't we?'

'*Touché*. But are you not concerned about your grandfather discovering who you are?'

'Unless you tell him I doubt there will be a problem.'

Unexpectedly Fitzroy grinned. For a moment his face lit up and he looked almost handsome. 'Bravo!' he said. 'I can tell you this, she was poisoned with arsenic.'

'How do you know?'

He crossed the room in three quick strides and put his finger to my lips. 'No questions. And remember to stay well away from my business.'

I swallowed and nodded. Fitzroy turned his back to me and went to gather up the papers. 'I suggest you wait a few moments before exiting the room to ensure no one sees us closeted together. Her Highness's reputation is damaged enough without daylight trysts under such serious circumstances.'

'I'm surprised you care.'

'Oh, I like her Highness very much,' said Fitzroy his hand on the door. 'Take care, Euphemia.'

A shudder ran through me. If Fitzroy was telling me to take care then things must be serious. I gave myself a mental shake. Everyone was making far too much of a state about this. It was quite simple: we had a murderer in the house, and I had to find him or her. My knees wobbled and I sat down hastily on a chair. And I had done everything to declare I would find him. The enormity of what I had done hit me. I had made myself a target, and this time neither Rory nor Bertram were in a position to help me.

Chapter Twenty

A Policeman's Lot

Dinner was a muted affair. Neither Richenda nor Bertram made an appearance. Everyone dutifully made conversation, but the topics of death and weddings were avoided. I learnt a lot about current London fashion and began to feel something of an interest despite myself. By the time the ladies rose to take tea spirits seem to be rising. We were all complicit in denying anything was amiss. I discovered it was a skill at which the upper classes excelled. 'Life goes on' was the unspoken motto.

Surrounded by the ancient wall of The Court I could in some ways understand this. Those present were all part of old families. Families who could trace their lineage back through various wars around the globe where various illustrious family members had lost limbs and lives. But despite whatever disasters befell them the families endured. Everyone took having an heir and spare extremely seriously.

'You're looking very serious, my dear,' said the

Countess coming to sit by me. 'And I was so trying to lighten the mood. Rather difficult when one has a body in the pantry.'

This comment won no answering smile from me. I felt the Countess's flippancy was wearing thin. She patted my hand. 'I'm sure Ratty will have it all sorted out by this evening. He's with the police person now. Then we can all get back to enjoying the wedding. After a quick funeral, of course. Lady Stapleford was French, wasn't she? Was she Catholic? Would she want bells and smells?'

'I'm sorry, did you say the police were here?'

'Don't worry, my dear. As I said Ratty is taking care of it all. You won't have to see them.'

'Excuse me,' I said rising hastily. 'I think I need a breath of fresh air.'

'Of course,' said the Countess. 'It is quite close in here. If you go along the west walk you should find the lilacs are in flower. They should smell divine tonight.'

I intercepted Robbins on his way to deliver further port to the dining room. 'Where is the Earl?'

'He is currently closeted with the police people, ma'am.'

'I know that, but where?'

Robbins's white eyebrows rose and there was a little pause. This was doubtless the closest he got to questioning a guest. 'I believe he is in his study.'

Two could play the waiting game, so I stood my ground.

'It is the third door on the left in the old east

wing corridor,' Robbins finally gave up. 'I believe he does not wish to be disturbed at present. Do the ladies require more tea? I would be more than happy to send one of the maids to attend to it.'

'What an excellent idea,' I said. Then I made my way quickly to the Earl's study before Robbins could get away to warn his master of my upcoming intrusion.

Whether one knocks, or not, before entering a room you know to be occupied, is a question that often confounds new staff and guests who aren't used to staying in great houses.

The answer is you never knock. If you intend to do something indiscreet or private in a room then there are ways of telegraphing this to your staff and a good butler should always anticipate such circumstances. If you have to knock, then you shouldn't be entering the room, is the basic answer. Therefore I acted like royalty, who of course have a right to go anywhere they please, and walked straight into the Earl's little conference.

Ratty sat behind a vast desk. Threep stood behind him and opposite on a small padded wooden chair sat a man in a long, plain, brown coat that the Earl wouldn't have given to his dog to lie on. He was a tall man and had folded uncomfortably into the chair. He clutched his hat between two shovel like hands.

When I entered he was leaning forward, while the Earl sat back in his seat very much at his ease.

I walked straight into the room. The Earl hesitated for a moment and then rose as he should to acknowledge my presence. 'Good evening,' I said addressing the room. 'I have just been informed the police have arrived and I thought as one of the few who has witnessed the original scene my testimony might be helpful.'

'And you are?' said the policeman unfolding himself from his chair to the extent his head almost touched the low ceiling of this old room.

I looked at the Earl. He coughed uncomfortably, but introduced me. The policeman bowed slightly. 'My wife will be amazed,' he said with a slow smile. I could see the Earl give a little grimace of distaste, but as I looked into the policeman's large brown eyes I had the fancy I saw shrewd intelligence there. 'Might I offer you my seat, ma'am?' he said.

'Thank you, no,' I said. 'It looks most uncomfortable.'

'A lady of great insight,' replied the policeman.

'We are almost finished,' said Ratty, attempting to head me off at the pass. 'We do not need to remind you of the sorry affairs this morning nor soil your ears with the details.'

'My ears are made of strong stuff, as is the rest of me,' I said. 'Perhaps, Threep, you could move the other chair from the corner for me to sit on?'

Threep glanced at the Earl, who remained standing and was doing his best craggy expression, and myself tall and cool. As a doctor he doubtless understood that in nature the female is more deadly than the male, or maybe it was simply my supposed superior standing, but I got my chair and everyone was seated once more.

'Now Inspector is it? What point had you reached?'

'Chief Inspector Brownly, Ma'am. The Earl here

informing me that the deceased, Lady Stapleford, was of a delicate constitution and found the consuming of oysters difficult to digest, but was sadly too polite to say so.'

'Then how does he know?' I challenged.

The inspector threw me a surprised, but grateful look.

'Her distant cousin, Renard Layfette, was able to give me the details,' said the Earl. His face and neck were absolutely rigid and his speech the most clipped I had ever heard. Here was a man unused to being challenged.

'But Renard was at the dining table. Surely, he would have noticed and said something? He was seated next to me and we had a clear view of Lady Stapleford.'

'Apparently,' said the Earl, 'he was too beguiled by his dinner companion to notice.' He turned to the chief inspector. 'Of course he regrets this bitterly, but is happy to give a written statement to you, Chief Inspector.'

'Renard Layfette has been out of the country for many years,' I said. 'This is his first return to England.'

'I believe,' said the Earl with a look so angry I was surprised his eyebrows didn't burst into flames, 'that it is an indisposition that stems from childhood.'

I gave a light laugh. 'I know Lady Stapleford was part French, but nevertheless it seems unlikely that any decent nursery nurse would give their young charges oysters.'

'Nevertheless,' began the Earl.

'Beside, surely the person to check this allergy

with is her son, Bertram.'

'He is too upset,' said the Earl through gritted teeth.

'To speak to the police about the murder of his mother?' I asked.

'Murder?' said Brownly. 'No one has suggested anything of the sort, Ma'am. I assure you.'

'But it is what I am suggesting, Chief Inspector. When Rory McLeod, the butler from Stapleford Hall, opened the door to Lady Stapleford's bed-chamber in the presence of Mrs Merion, the housekeeper and myself, Lady Stapleford's body was contorted in pain and the room was in considerable disarray.'

'All pointing to death by reaction to food, eh doctor?' said the Earl.

'Um,' said Threep.

'Then explain the empty cup on the floor? The saucer was broken, but the cup in which was presented the bedtime drink was drunk dry. A woman already in the throes of distress from a food allergy would not be likely to drain such a drink, would she, doctor?'

'It depends,' said Threep, edging back towards the window with a hunted expression on his face.

'Could it not also be that her demeanour and the amount of vomit present in the room could also be indicative of arsenic poisoning?' I turned to the inspector. 'I once had a cat that ate some poison which had been left out for the rats.'

'Lady Stapleford was not a cat!' said the Earl. 'This is nonsense.'

'No, she was a human being and thus a mammal. One might expect similar symptoms.'

'If there is any doubt,' said Brownly, 'I will have to ask for an autopsy.'

'We do not cut up our dead,' said the Earl springing to his feet. 'Let me make that quite clear.'

'She isn't actually a member of your family,' I said. 'As far as I am aware she is only related to you in the sense that most of the noble households of England and France are distantly related. Very distantly.'

'I think I should speak to her son after all, your grace,' said Brownly. The Earl opened his mouth to speak. The police inspector also rose. 'I am afraid I must insist.'

The Earl sank back down into his chair. 'Ring the bell, Threep, and summon Robbins. It seems we have to disturb the grieving son.'

Robbins came in with an apologetic look on his face rather akin to an ancient Labrador that been digging up the prize flowerbeds. 'I believe Mr Bertram Stapleford is in the pantry,' he said grimly. 'Sitting with his mother.'

'Coldest place in the house,' said Threep to Brownly.

'It can't be helped,' said the Earl. 'The chief inspector wishes to speak to him. I think the word he used was "insisted".'

'Certainly, Your Grace.'

An uneasy silence settled in the room. Brownly turned his hat over and over in hands. The Earl harrumphed into his moustache and Threep tried unsuccessfully to perch on the windowsill. It was small and hard and he had to, as it were, keep turning the other cheek.

The door flew open and Bertram stormed in. His hair was wildly out of place, his eyes red and his face a sick greyish pallor. It looked as if he had slept in his suit and perhaps he had.

'You are the police?' he said addressing Brownly. 'Chief Inspector Brow–'

Bertram cut him off. 'Then I want to know what the devil you think you're about!'

The Earl stood. 'My dear chap, I am so sorry. Threep, get Mr Stapleford a seat.'

The doctor looked around the small room helplessly.

'I don't need a seat,' snapped Bertram. 'I want to know what's going on.'

The Earl put out his hands in a placating manner. 'Just a small misunderstanding,' he said. 'The chief inspector and I were about to agree this was an unfortunate reaction to the oysters when her Highness here came in and claimed it was murder.'

'What?' said Bertram, his head whipping round to face me, an intense expression in his brown eyes.

'I know, dear fellow. I know,' said the Earl. He lowered his voice, so he could pretend I wouldn't hear though we both knew I would, 'Young women can be prone to these fantasies.'

Bertram's eyes met my squarely. 'Fantasies,' he cried. 'Of course my mother was bloody murdered! Euphemia was right!'

'And who is this Euphemia?' asked Brownly.

'I have no idea,' said the Earl. Slowly, everyone's gaze turned towards me.

143

Chapter Twenty-one

Of Cats, Rats and Dowagers

'A maid,' I said. 'A maid from Stapleford Hall.'

'Ring the bell, Threep, and we'll get Robbins to get this well-informed maid in here.'

Bertram rolled his eyes at me helplessly.

'You'll have to get him to ask for Merry,' I said, thinking on my feet, 'She's called that for short.'

'I should think so,' said the Earl. 'No decent household would hire a maid called Euphemia. Most unsuitable.'

All too quickly Merry was brought into the room. As usual she seemed to shrink when surrounded by the people from upstairs. She bobbed a curtsey to the Earl, but edged subtly my way. I guessed she wanted moral support. I wanted to be able to whisper to her.

'I understand you found Lady Stapleford,' said the Earl not even bothering with her name.

'Yes, your Grace,' said Merry in restrained voice.

'And you were the one who first cried murder? That is correct, isn't it Euphemia?'

Merry whirled to face me. Her eyes were wide as saucers. 'Don't be concerned, Euphemia,' I said. 'The Earl only wants to know the truth.'

'The truth!' said Merry looking for all the world as if someone had smacked her in the head

144

with a kipper.

'Why you thought her Ladyship had been murdered,' said Bertram.

Merry's eyes went even wider until I was sure they were in danger of popping out. Then she took a deep breath, shot me a look of pure malice and turned back to face the Earl. 'That would be the rats, sir.'

'Rats?' said Brownly.

Merry, who had managed not to notice the overly large policeman crouched in the chair, rocked backwards. He gave her a friendly smile. The edges of Merry's mouth lifted slightly. 'Yes rats. I were brought up on my uncle's farm, seeing as there were too many of us for Ma to keep in London, and he were always putting it down for the rats. Arsenic. Affects creatures very cruelly I think.' Her voice became a little stronger at the end. Merry was at her most forthright when expressing her opinions.

'Rats! Cats!' spluttered the Earl. 'Surely young woman you are not comparing Lady Stapleford to a rat?'

I could almost see the hackles on Merry's back rising, so I interrupted before she could utter some of her more liberal views. 'Isn't this for the doctor to judge?'

'Well, Dr Threep, could the symptoms both these young ladies have been describing be caused by arsenic poisoning?' asked Chief Inspector Brownly.

The doctor stuck a finger under his collar and pulled. His glasses made another bid to escape and he only just caught them in time.

'Well, Doctor,' said the Earl.

'Yes, Doctor, what is your opinion?' asked Bertram.

'Er,' said Threep, 'I couldn't be sure unless I did an autopsy and Lord Stapleford has assured me that will not be happening.'

'That's my decision not his,' said the chief inspector, rising to his full height. 'Now give us your answer.'

The unfortunate doctor slumped against the window. 'It's possible,' he said.

'Threep,' snapped the Earl.

'I simply can't tell,' said the doctor, 'without an autopsy.'

The chief inspector turned his attention to Bertram. 'You, sir, also seem to believe it was murder. Do you have any suggestions as to who might have been your mother's assailant or even why she might have attracted the attentions of a poisoner?'

'I have no idea how the mind of a poisoner might work,' snapped Bertram. 'If you're asking me did my mother have any enemies present in this house I am aware she and her cousin Renard Layfette have a long running feud since before my birth.'

'This would be the same Layfette as you was offering to sign a document that Lady Stapleford was allergic to oysters, Your Grace?' asked Brownly.

'Rubbish!' cried Bertram. 'My mother is part French. She has eaten oysters all her life!'

Chief Inspector Brownly took a step towards the Earl's desk. 'It seems to me that this matter is not

146

as clear-cut as was first assumed. I shall send a police ambulance to take Lady Stapleford's body away and request the coroner to issue an order for an autopsy. Can I ask that no one leaves the Court, neither family nor staff, nor the guests. As it is quite late tonight I shall return tomorrow with my sergeant and we will began conducting interviews so this event can be cleared up as quickly as possible.'

'I shall telephone the Chief Constable!' declared the Earl.

'Please do so, your Grace,' said Brownly. 'I shall be speaking to him myself.' He put his hat back on his head, nodded to the assembled company and asked Robbins if he would be so kind as to show him the way to the exit. Robbins complied if for no other reason than to get away from the Earl whose face was turning puce with rage.

As soon as they had departed the Earl shouted at Merry, 'Get back to your work, girl. I will be speaking to your master.' Merry picked up her skirts and fled. 'And as for you Threep, call yourself a doctor? You're a quack. A tuppenny-ha'penny saw bones. I'll see you never work in this area again. You idiot of a man. You scraggy good for nothing... These people are going to hanging around my house for days now and we've still got that damn blasted wedding.'

Bertram coughed loudly. 'I am sorry my mother's death has put you to so much inconvenience, Your Grace,' he said in an icy voice. 'Rest assured I want my mother away from the Court and safely home in our chapel as soon as possible. However, I will not stand by and let her murderer

147

go free in order to allow your celebrations to go unhindered. With reflection I am sure you will appreciate my point of view!' And so saying he turned his back to the Earl and offered me his arm. I was more than happy to make my escape by his side.

Chapter Twenty-two

For Whom the Bell Didn't Toll

Bertram kept up a smart pace until we gained the terrace. Tactfully I steered him along the west walk. The clouds above us burned with a rosy glow from the dying light of the sun and the scent of lilacs was indeed heady in the air. The grassy terrace rolled away to our west and in the distance we could hear the sweet sound of the fountain. In other circumstances it would have been a most wonderful and possibly romantic evening, but beside me I could feel Bertram trembling with rage.

'I am so sorry,' I said.

Bertram stopped and turned to face me. 'I owe you an apology, Euphemia. I should never have questioned your judgment.'

'You were in shock. And quite naturally so.'

Bertram made his way to a seat under a weeping willow and handed me into a seat. I could hardly see the house and I realised he had done this deliberately. My heart, usually a reliable organ, began to run somewhat faster.

'I did not wish to think anyone could so dislike Mama that they might actually do her harm,' said Bertram.

'No, of course not,' I said gently.

'Will you stop interrupting, Euphemia,' said Bertram shortly, quite in his old style. This drew an involuntarily smile from me. Bertram broke into a grin. 'You were far easier to handle as a housekeeper. Not that you were that easy then either,' he said. 'Now, you're royalty...'

'I'm still Euphemia St John.'

'I don't know,' said Bertram. His eyes appraised me, not in the way Richard Stapleford might, but as one seeing an old friend in a new guise. 'You play the part of the lady as if you were born to it. Who were your parents? You have never told me.'

'My father was a country vicar,' I said. 'My mother had some,' I paused trying to think of the right word, 'connections. It was her aim to teach me to behave like a lady. Quite out of my station.'

'She did a bloody good job,' said Bertram frankly. 'If I'd never met you before I wouldn't question twice that you were this high-faluting friend of Richenda's. Though I'm afraid that's all going to come out now.'

'I hope not,' I said. 'It would be disastrous for Richenda and her wedding as much as myself. I had hoped that I might be able to solve the crime before any awkward questions were asked.'

Bertram began to laugh. It started as a slow chuckle, but within a few minutes he had flung back his head and given way to mirth. I began to fear he had become hysterical and was summoning the courage to slap him, when he suddenly sat upright and wiped the tears from his eyes. 'Has anyone ever told you, Euphemia, that you are one in a million. No, one in a trillion!'

'I believe I am a little out of the norm,' I said as graciously as I could.

Bertram put his hand on my arm. 'Don't! Don't,' he said. 'You'll set me off again. Now you must have a plan of action. What is it?'

'Not so much a plan, as I've been going over things again and again in my mind and some pieces don't add up.'

'Explain,' demanded Bertram, giving me his full attention.

'Well, Merry is checking who delivered the bed time drinks and how they were delivered. It seems the maid who is often assigned to our corridor, Lucy, is very shy and has been known to leave drinks outside the door.'

'Where anyone might tamper with them,' said Bertram.

'Exactly. We know that your mother, Richenda and I had all retired to bed before many of the men.'

'Richard and Tipton had that awful row in the billiard room.'

'When was that?' I asked. 'Because Tipton came by our rooms, very drunk and making some silly remarks about the wedding. He even invited Merry to spend one of his last nights of freedom with him.'

'He must have been three sheets to the wind,' said Bertram. 'Was Richenda in the room?'

'I said he was drunk, not an imbecile.'

Bertram acknowledged this with a wry twist of his lips. 'I would guess then that he came down and got into the argument later. I wonder why he didn't simply head off to bed?'

'Something must have happened,' I said. 'Something must have made him feel that he had to search out Richard there and then.'

'What on Earth could be that urgent,' said Bertram.

'Don't men in their cups often think the most ridiculous things are urgent?'

'Yes.' Bertram sighed. 'And while he isn't exactly an imbecile, Tipton is not that smart.'

'But all this conjecture, though worth considering, only comes together when Merry gets the information on the drinks delivery.'

'When will that be?'

'I'm hoping when she comes to my room tonight.'

Bertram nodded. 'I shall do my best to get there discreetly.'

Several comments came to the tip of my tongue, but this was Bertram's mother and I could hardly shut him out of my investigations. Besides we had worked well as a team before. 'There is one thing that has been bothering me,' I said. 'Why didn't your mother ring the bell when she felt herself becoming ill?'

'Perhaps she was in too much pain,' said Bertram, his eyes clouding.

'It's right beside the bed.'

'You think no one answered?' said Bertram shocked.

'As I understand the servants are shut in,

locked in, to a separate part of the building that is only connected by a single corridor.'

'No,' said Bertram, 'the servants wouldn't have retired to their section of the house while so many guests were around. What's more, the bells run across to their quarters, and even if that didn't work Robbins stays on this side. All the bells are routed past him at night, so he, at least, would have heard it.'

'Is he a sound sleeper?'

'You can be assured that the Earl makes sure his bells are loud,' said Bertram.

'Then the other reason she couldn't have summoned help,' I said.

'Would be if the bell had been disconnected,' finished Bertram.

We looked at each other. 'Rory has the key to the bedroom,' I said.

'But how do we know that's the only key?' asked Bertram. 'Most houses this large have spares or even master keys.'

'We need to check that room now,' I said, 'before anyone gets a chance to undo their handy work.'

'I agree. If the bell isn't working then it's more weight to our suspicion that my mother was murdered.'

I stood up. 'Let's go and find Rory,' I said.

Chapter Twenty-three

Man and Master

'No, I will go into the house and summon Robbins, who will send Rory out to meet us in the west walk,' said Bertram.

'But wouldn't it be quicker...' I began.

'He's a servant, Euphemia and you are a lady. There is no question of you chasing after a manservant, let alone going below stairs to find him.'

'Won't Robbins think it odd?'

'Robbins is paid an excellent wage to serve, not think. This is how servants normally operate.'

I was left alone wondering how my future husband was going to take to being summoned to meet Bertram and I in the shrubbery. How I could ever face Robbins again I simply did not know. There are times when I am very grateful that we have not developed the ability to read one another's minds. I allow it might be useful discovering truth but the endless mortification makes that a doubtful positive.

Bertram returned quickly. He was breathing heavily. I bade him sit down and recover himself, and crossed my fingers that Rory would not arrive before he had recovered his composure.

Luck was not on my side. Rory appeared running across the terrace from the house. He was by my side in moments.

'What's wrong?' he asked me. Then he noticed the panting Bertram, not at my feet, but on the seat beside me. 'Euphemia?' he queried, turning my name into a suspicious and angry enquiry.

'Good, McLeod, you're here,' said Bertram. 'We need your help.'

'Indeed, sir,' said Rory, rolling his Rs in an alarming manner.

'Sorry,' said Bertram, 'you'll need to give me a moment to catch my breath.' He pressed his hand to his chest and inhaled deeply. I sat down beside him at once. 'Are you quite well, Bertram?' I asked. He gave me a small smile through his laboured breathing. 'I think recent events have taken it out of me a bit. Got a bit of a dodgy ticker.'

'Then perhaps you should be more careful in the activities you indulge in – sir,' said Rory.

I stood heavily on his foot. 'Mr Bertram and I have discussing his mother's murder. We believe that the bell in the room may have been tampered with. Do you still have the key to the room?'

'Aye, Mrs Merion wanted it back, but I only had to mention that the police would be wanting a word when she decided it would it be better for a man to have it, and especially a man from the Stapleford household.'

'Very clever,' said Bertram. His breathing was easing now. 'Do you know if there are any other keys for the same room?'

'I asked,' said Rory, 'Mrs Merion seemed unsure. The wing you are referring to is part of the

154

oldest section of the building.'

'So there have been keys knocking around for longer than she has been in post,' I said. 'I'm always surprised that these sorts of old houses are not burgled more often, they have such a lackaday attitude to security.' Rory gave me a funny look.

'Will you accompany us to the room, McLeod,' said Bertram. 'We need to check if the bell is working.'

'Then you'd better take the key and I'll head down the servants quarters to see if it rings. Give me ten minutes then ring. I'll come up to the room and tell you what's happened.' Bertram grew a shade paler, but nodded.

We arrived outside the room and were immediately aware of a gentle snoring sound. 'Can Richenda still be asleep?' I asked. 'Dr Threep gave her a sedative, but that was hours ago.' Bertram's hand was shaking as he fitted the key into the lock. 'I damn well hope it's her. I don't fancy being haunted by my mother's ghost. She had a devil of a temper.'

I checked up and down the corridor. It was empty. We stepped inside and closed the door behind us. I immediately noticed the smell of lavender: as well as removing the bedding, the whole room had been thoroughly cleaned. Lady Stapleford's cases rested at the foot of her bed. I opened one of the wardrobe doors. It was empty. Even all her things has been packed up. 'Someone has been here before us.' I said a little unnecessarily. 'I imagine they will also have fixed the bell.'

Bertram consulted his watch. He rang the bell.

155

We waited. Neither of us felt comfortable enough to sit in this room. What seemed like a very long time later, there a brief knock on the door and Rory entered. 'Nothing,' he said. 'Not a sound.'

'So whoever had this room cleaned didn't know the bell wasn't working,' said Bertram.

'It was probably the Countess.' I said. 'I tried to persuade her to leave the bedding alone. She must have decided she couldn't bear to leave the room uncleaned.'

'It is high summer,' said Rory. 'Without wishing to be indelicate, the smell would have quickly reached the other rooms. I'm sorry, sir, but the room was very bad.'

'I guessed,' said Bertram. 'They had tried to clean Mama up before I...' he sagged suddenly. Rory caught him. 'I think we'd better be getting you to your room, sir. Maybe you could find out if that doctor is still on the premises, Euphemia?'

'There's no need to fuss,' said Bertram. He tried to pull away from Rory and stand unsupported. He collapsed on the bed. 'Euphemia!' said Rory.

'I'm on my way,' I said. I hurried to my room and rang the bell. To my surprise Robbins answered my call instead of Merry. 'Can I be of assistance, your Highness,' he said with the look of dread on his face that only a man who fears he is about to be confronted with the workings of women's intimate apparel can conjure. I told him briefly that Bertram was being taken to his room and needed a doctor.

'Not sickness, I hope your Highness,' said Robbins.

'His heart,' I said shortly.

156

'Thank goodness for that,' said Robbins. 'Begging your Highness's pardon, but Cook would be in a right taking...'

'Now, please, Robbins,' I said in my most authoritative voice. The butler bowed till his nose almost touched his knee and then scurried away as fast as it was possible for him to do without actually breaking into an undignified sprint.

I sat down on my bed overcome by fatigue. No one had drawn my curtains and I could see night sending the shadowy fingers of dusk across the sky. I hadn't had the chance to ask how the bell mechanism might have been disabled, but Rory had locked the room again when he left with Bertram, so I would have to wait until tomorrow. I wanted Merry to help me out of my dress, but I did not wish to summon Robbins again. I had been too preoccupied thinking of Bertram to ask why he had answered my summons. I hoped Merry hadn't got herself into hot water asking questions.

I moved across to the chair by the window. From here I could see much of the grounds, which were undeniably lovely. I would rest my head against the batwings of the chair and wait. Merry would know I needed her and would come to me as soon as she could. I found I was crossing my fingers for Bertram. There had always been whispers that he wasn't entirely fit, but Richard had often poo-poohed them as him simply being cosseted by his mother. I had fallen into the error of thinking this to be so too. I had never seen him become ill though on the very first occasion we met I remember him and Richard discussing his ill health. Was it because they shared a common failing that he had been so attracted to Miss Wilton? My eyes felt hot and prickly. Surely he would not share her fate?

I sat staring out of the window, seeing nothing and thinking of all the times Bertram and I had worked, argued and laughed together.

At some point fatigue must have over taken me, because the next thing I knew the room was full dark, except for the embers glowing in the remnants of the fire. The hair on the back of my neck was up and I was completely awake. Something had startled me from my slumbers, but what was it?

I had a creeping sensation I was not alone. Being accompanied in a darkened room has become all too frequent an occurrence in my life since I began working for the Staplefords, so I was not as panicked as one might expect for a virtuous young woman.

Firstly, I deliberately slowed my breathing, so any would be assailant, or more optimistically burglar, would think me still asleep. Secondly, I listened very, very carefully and thirdly, I did my best to bring to mind mentally the contents of the room and any ready weapons there might be to hand. The best I could conceive of at the present was the heavy hair brush on the dressing table to my left. To my right there was also a small table with a vase, but I was less confident of grabbing that with a first lunge in the dark.

A part of me hoped it was Merry, sneaking in late to attend to her maidly duties, but I could think of no reason why she would not have brought a candle to light her way.

My hidden companion must have noticed a change in my breathing when I initially awoke and frozen for now I heard the outward sigh of someone who has been holding their breath. So this was not Merry.

I continued to listen though now my heart was pounding so hard in my chest that I was surprised it had not awoken the entire household. A footstep fell. Whoever this was was moving very, very slowly and carefully. Perhaps it was a burglar. A member of royalty might have been thought to have sufficient jewels in her room to risk incursion. But then they too would have needed some light to work by.

A further footstep fell. The direction was undoubtedly towards me. Time expanded. My brain sped through reasons why the intruder might not wish me harm and found none. Another footfall. My only chance was to take them unaware. I flexed my muscles ready for action. Another footfall. They were almost upon me.

I stood quickly and took a step towards where I believed the hairbrush to be, but in getting up and turning my senses had become confused. I stepped straight into the arms of my assailant.

Chapter Twenty-four

Encounters in the Dark

Arms like steel wrapped around me. My assailant lifted me bodily off my feet and threw me onto the bed. I immediately rolled off onto the floor. Not a moment before the figure too fell on the bed. He, for no woman could surely be strong enough, gave a low growl of anger. I pushed my way under the bed, but he was quick. He landed on the floor in seconds and caught on to my ankle with cruelly gripping fingers. I lashed out, hoping to find a leg of the bed to hold onto, but only darkness met my hand. He pulled me backwards. I turned and twisted trying to grasp the underneath of the mattress. Anything. I was terrified of his intentions.

He almost had me clear of the bed when my hand finally snagged on something cool and cold. I grabbed it as I was pulled roughly from my cover. He still had his grip on my ankle. Now he moved it higher, to my thigh, at the same time pinioning my right arm. It was due to nothing other than pure luck that I had grabbed my weapon with my left hand. Now clear of the mattress I brought the chamber pot down hard upon his head. It smashed into a thousand pieces and his grip loosened. I pushed upward hard with a strength I didn't know I possessed and threw his body from mine while he lay dazed.

160

I staggered towards the door, but again my senses betrayed me. I crashed into the small table in the opposite direction and set it rocking wildly. My eyes were used enough to the dark that I could grab at the imperilled vase upon it. I turned and hurled towards my assailant. He must have just gained his feet for from the sound of it my vase hit him mid-section. Then finally I managed to draw enough breath and screamed as loudly as I could.

This was the final straw for my assailant. I heard him wrench open the door and then the sound of running footsteps. Light from the corridor flooded into the room. I staggered over to the door and leant against the frame. I could see no sign of anyone. In the harshness of the light I became aware of my torn dress and my hair hanging around my face.

I turned on the gaslight and returned to sit by the fire. I picked up the poker. It seemed to have a life of its own as I prodded at the fire. I realised my hands were shaking. I pulled the coverlet from my bed and wrapped myself into a cocoon. I settled down to wait for Merry or the morning whichever came first. I had no intention of falling asleep. In fact I doubted I would ever be capable of sleep again.

I had poked the fire back into life three more times before there was a scratch at my door and Merry popped her head in. 'Cor,' she said, 'you'll never believe the night I've had.'

I took one look at her friendly face and burst into tears. Immediately Merry was crouched by my side her arms around me. She saw my appearance clearly for the first time.

'Dear God in Heaven,' she exclaimed. 'What has 'appened to you?'

I gave vent to many sobs and cries before I was ready to able to tell her the whole sorry tale. 'And 'e didn't do you no other 'arm?' she said seriously, her hands cupping my face. 'You can tell me, Euphemia. I'll look after yer.'

This, of course, brought on another bout of weeping, but I was able to assure her that my attacker had done no more than bruise and frighten me. 'I think he did intend more,' I hiccupped, 'but the weight of the chamber pot on his head took his mind off it. Thank goodness the Earl and Countess are so old-fashioned.' I tried to summon up a weak smile.

'I only wish the damned thing had been full,' said Merry, 'or a shard of it had gone deep into him and done mortal harm.' She rocked back on her heels. 'Have you any idea who it was?'

I shook my head. 'He didn't speak.'

'Right,' said Merry and stood up. 'I'm going to get some help to hunt this bastard down.'

'Wait! No!' I stood up quickly and found my legs were not yet back to their normal strength. I wobbled into the small table which overturned. Merry hurried to help me sit.

'What are you on about Euphemia? No one's safe while's a manic abroad.'

'But the police will want to investigate. They will want to ask me questions.'

Merry took a seat on the other side of the fire. 'This bloody daft scheme of the Staplefords is going to tie our hands, isn't it?'

'I can't risk them uncovering my identity,' I said with more truth than Merry knew.

'But we can't do nothink!' exclaimed Merry. 'I'm going to go and wake up Robbins, even if it does cause a rumpus, and get back into the servants' quarters. Rory needs to know.'

'What happened to you?' I asked.

'Nothink important,' said Merry, in that offhand voice she has when she's got herself into trouble.

'No,' I insisted, 'tell me. It might be important.'

'Oh, it's just that Merrit and I were out admiring views and we got locked out.'

'You and your views,' I said and this time it really did bring a faint smile to my lips. 'But didn't you watch the time?'

'Of course we did. Some bugger locked the door from the garden earlier than they should have done. Probably someone having a joke.'

'Or someone trying to make sure that you weren't with me when they came to visit.'

'But I could have roused Robbins to get in.'

'But you didn't. Someone knew you well enough to know you'd try to find your own solution rather than cause a disturbance. How did you get back in?'

'One of the cellars into the kitchen was open. Merrit's down there now.'

'Right!' said Merry, 'I'll tell you what we'll do and I ain't brooking no argument.'

Which is how Merry came to be sleeping on a makeshift bed with poor Merrit standing guard outside my door for the rest of the night. He was

163

under firm instructions to get himself away before the morning maids came round.

Merry slept with a kitchen knife, provided by Merrit, under her pillow.

Chapter Twenty-five

The Penetrating Light of Morning

Merry told me firmly I had passed a restless night and would not be down to breakfast. 'But I'm hungry,' I said.

'Great romantic heroine you'd make. You should still be weeping and wailing and instead you're demanding toast.'

'Eggs and sausages, please.'

Merry sighed. 'I'll try and smuggle them up. Delicate young ladies who sleep badly don't demand pig in the morning.'

'Thanks, Merry,' I said.

'And I'm bringing Rory to come and see you.'

'Oh no!' I cried.

'Would you rather I fetch Mr Bertram?'

I flung myself back against my pillow, accidentally discovering some bruises that had previously not made themselves known. 'Fine. Rory's better than Bertram. Bertram would be storming about the place before we could stop him.'

'At least tell him the full story before you bring him up,' I begged. 'I don't want to go through it all again.'

'Let him kill the messenger,' she said pouting. 'Very well. But you stay right there in bed and if anyone other than Rory or I come through that door you scream blue murder!'

I nodded. 'I don't think anyone will try an attack in broad daylight.'

'Depends how desperate they are,' and with this comforting thought Merry left me alone.

I spent my time waiting for them to return reconstructing as much as I could remember of last night. My memory was already playing me tricks and in daylight I had trouble working out what had happened where. I thought hard about my assailant, but by the time they returned I had only remembered one thing.

'He'd been drinking whisky,' I said as Rory entered. 'I didn't focus on it at the time–' the rest of my sentence was lost as he enfolded me in a bear hug. Over his shoulder I saw Merry's face split in a delighted grin. 'Shall I leave you two alone then?' she asked cheekily.

Rory ignored her. 'Are you certain you have taken no serious harm, my bonnie lass?' I looked up into those luminous green eyes and felt safe. Relief flooded through me and I buried my face in his jacket. 'I'm sure,' I said in a muffled voice.

'Come in and close that door, Merry,' said Rory, 'where you born in a barn?'

'Just trying not to intrude,' said Merry.

'Well, so you know Euphemia and I are engaged. Once this nonsense is all over we'll be getting married.'

'Rory,' I breathed.

'Aye, I know we said we wouldn't tell anyone

165

yet,' said Rory, 'but Merry can keep a secret.' I pulled away from him and gave him a dubious look. 'Aye well, she'll keep a secret if she wants to keep her position,' he said.

'Does Mr Bertram know?' she asked and I could have happily thrown the vase at her head if it hadn't already been broken.

'So do you have any idea who it was?' asked Rory. 'It's a gent I'm gey keen to meet!'

'I don't think it was Tipton,' I said. 'He's lighter and we know that he's a deadly assailant.'

'Do we?' asked Merry.

'It was most likely him that did for Mrs Wilson,' said Rory shortly, ignoring Merry's sharp intake of breath. 'And don't you go spreading that around. If there'd be enough proof I'd have seen the man hang.'

'I think it was someone who wasn't used to fighting,' I said. 'I had to struggle hard, but I did get away.'

'Hmm,' said Rory, 'so not our highland friend then?'

'Definitely not,' I said. 'Besides he'd have no reason.'

'Who?' asked Merry lost. 'Muller?'

Rory ignored her again, 'You said that he smelled of whisky?'

'You're thinking it might have been an impulse? But whoever it was bribed someone to lock Merry and Merrit out.'

'And they knew about Merry and Merrit more to the point,' said Rory. 'It's got to be one of the Staplefords or their close associates.'

'Turns out Bertram is ill in bed,' said Merry,

desperate to join in.

'Heartache is it,' growled Rory darkly. 'Maybe I should go and check on him.'

I put a restraining hand on his arm. 'Don't be daft,' I said.

'When I think of the times I've found you and that man in close confines,' said Rory. 'It's clear he has a partiality for you. I'm thinking that perhaps with the drink his desire got the better of him.'

'Word below stairs is that it's his heart,' said Merry.

'You saw how bad he was yesterday,' I said.

'Well, maybe,' said Rory. 'But I'm not ruling him out. You're not to be alone with the man again, Euphemia. I forbid it.'

Merry raised her eyes to heaven, but all I said was, 'So we are agreed my attacker knew us, the Stapleford household, well and decided to take his chances and try to...' I stopped at a loss for words.

'I think there's no doubt he would have killed you in the end,' said Merry. 'Whoever he was he wouldn't want you running the risk of remembering anything about him.'

'So we need you to find out which of the gentlemen were drunk last night, Rory. And you Merry to find out who was bribed to lock you and Merrit out.'

'I'll be doing that alright,' said Merry in a voice that boded ill for the culprit if she caught them.

'I need to make an appearance at lunch. If the attacker knows who I really am then he'll know why I haven't made a fuss and if he doesn't then it'll throw him off guard.'

'You want to see how people react to you,' said Rory.

'Yes.'

'That's gey dangerous.'

'As dangerous as sitting up here alone in my room? The interesting thing must be he thinks I know something about the murder. I was the one who insisted the police investigate,' I admitted, 'but they've agreed. Killing me would only make that investigation more serious.'

'Unless he knew who you were and had no intention of killing you, but only...' Rory couldn't bring himself to say the word.

'Punishing me? Warning me?' I suggested, 'which would also mean he thinks I know something important about Lady Stapleford's death.'

'Do you?' asked Merry.

'I don't think so. Bertram, Rory and I discovered last night that her bell had been disconnected, which is why she didn't call for help. Well, she probably did, but no one heard her.'

'How horrible,' said Merry, whitening. 'She was a difficult mistress, but no one deserves to die like that.'

'Think Euphemia, think,' urged Rory, 'what else do you and you alone know.'

'That someone else might know?' I quailed inwardly. Would my grandfather, if he was made aware of who I was, send someone to kill me rather than deal with a family scandal?

'What?' asked Rory being far too perceptive.

'I can only think that I saw Richenda and Lady Stapleford fighting. Maybe someone thinks I

168

heard more of their discussion than I did.'

'What did you hear?' asked Rory,

'Probably less than Merry. By the time we got there it was all name-calling, hair-pulling and shrieking.'

'They were that angry with each other?' said Rory aghast. 'Hair-pulling? Yer not pulling my leg?'

'No,' said Merry, 'They were fair laying into each other.'

'Well, we've both got our tasks, so I think it's time for Euphemia to do something – publicly, and without danger – and ask Richenda what that argument was all about.'

'You think she'll tell me?' I said. 'She hates me.'

'If you're going to stay alive,' said Merry bluntly, 'we need to find out what the hell is going on.'

Chapter Twenty-six

The Blushing Bride (Again)

Moments after I left Merry I realised I had forgotten to ask her what she had discovered from Lucy, the shy evening drink producer, but it was too late now. My stomach growled and the second and last warning bell for luncheon rang.

Knowing Richenda's love of food I decided to approach her after lunch. But again I found the lunch was an informal buffet affair. I found this odd. It is normal to expect to serve oneself at breakfast, but not at luncheon. Of course, it is dinner that is the big occasion, and the meal one is expected to dress for, but still... As I surveyed the full room, people hovering around the loaded tables like pigs around a feeding trough, I observed two things. Firstly, death gives one an appetite. This does not fit right with the strictures of being a lady, but food reminds us we are alive and can still enjoy earthly pleasures. The men present had no hesitation in piling up their plates again and again. My second observation was that the senior members of the party, the two Earls and the Countess, were not present.

Tipton's mother sat with a heaped plate of asparagus spears her gaze far into the distance as she chewed, and if truth be said she looked decided bovine. There was no sign of Tippy's father. Richenda had withdrawn slightly and was half hidden behind some plants, at a small secondary table. I gathered my portion of food and moved over to join her.

'May I join you?'

Richenda made a snorting sound. I decided to take this as a yes. I sat down beside her and said quietly, 'As I am your good friend and bridesmaid it would be remiss of me not to offer what solace I can.'

'You're playing your part well,' said Richenda between mouthfuls. 'Too damn well if we're not careful. I've already had a couple of the men trying to sound me out to see if you're available. Even Tip-top, Tippy's eldest brother asked.' She raised her fork close to my face. 'Don't,' she said waggling it for emphasis, 'get ideas. A liaison with

170

any of this men would shatter our charade and marriage with any of them would be out of the question.'

I coloured slightly. 'While the lady I am impersonating might not be adverse to secret trysts, I was brought up quite differently.'

'You are out of your class.'

'If that is what it means to be out of my class then I am very happy there!' I said with some heat.

Richenda paused and put her cutlery down. 'I don't know what to make of you,' she said frankly, 'my brother tells me such tales of you and Bertram is obviously smitten, but then at the slightest whiff of intimate matters you turn positively pious. If it's an act it's a very good one.'

It was one the tip of my tongue to say I was nothing but what I appeared to be, but this was untrue on so many levels. Instead I said, 'Come let us not quarrel. We both find ourselves in a difficult situation. I do not fancy being closely questioned by the police and I am sure you wish to proceed with the wedding as soon as possible. Have Amelia or the Countess proposed anything?'

'They want the funeral first, of course, but seeing as we are all gathered together and the banns were read here, they want to get it over with.'

'So it won't be on your birthday?'

'Unlikely, but seeing as I've said you have to return to your own country in two weeks, I'm hoping that will carry things along.'

'Goodness, Richenda, if you are going to say things like that you must also tell me!'

'I just did. Don't get stroppy with me. I'm a lady

and you're nothing but a jumped-up scrubber.'

'A jumped-up scrubber who could drop you and your precious twin in a great deal of trouble,' I snapped back.

'Ooh, so the worm turns does it? Don't doubt for a moment who would come out on top if any revelations were made!'

I took a deep breath and bit down hard on a piece of celery. I find celery is a most useful vegetable for venting your anger. 'Look, the police will be interviewing us all today...'

'They've started,' said Richenda. 'I've already done my bit.'

'I was going to say if there are any more – er – issues that you don't want revealed, now might be the time to forewarn me.'

'Like?'

'Like my needing to know I am unavailable in two weeks' time. Or say why you and Lady Stapleford were arguing so fiercely?'

It was not the subtlest of approaches, but I simply couldn't think of how to ask the question other than in a straight forward manner. As it was, my approach fell awry.

'Are you trying to blackmail me?' said Richenda with a positive growl in her voice.

'No, of course not. The police must have asked you about it already.'

'It wasn't mentioned.'

'I wonder why not? I wasn't the only one to notice the disturbances a lot of the servants knew about it too.'

'Who are the police going to take the word of? A lady or a maid?'

172

'It's not that easy,' I said carefully, 'I think the police will try and avoid questioning either of the Earls or the Countess, but I think they will be less discriminating with everyone else. If perhaps there was something I could let drop in my interview that explained the friction, it would make things easier.'

I often dismiss Richenda as unintelligent, but she has a certain calculating ability, even if it is far inferior to her brothers'. She gazed into the distance for a while. Then she said, 'You could tell them that my stepmother had qualms that Tippy wasn't good enough for me and that being passionately in love with him, and also almost on the eve of my wedding, I was vastly affronted.'

'Is it true?' I asked. 'Didn't she want you to marry Tippy?'

'No, she didn't, but she chose a fine time to tell me. Yes, we argued and she said some foul things about him that sent me almost mad with rage, but she is only my stepmama. I do not need her permission to wed, so you can assure the police I had no reason to kill her.'

'Foul things?'

'Nothing that bears repeating,' said Richenda. I think the old cow was losing her mind. Whoever got rid of her did us all a favour.'

'You never said that to the police!' I exclaimed.

'No, of course I didn't. What I want to know is what you are up to? If you hadn't cried murder this would all have been tidied up in no time at all.'

'There were already suspicions,' I said thinking of Fitzroy.

'Come closer,' said Richenda, 'Smile. People are watching us. Let them think we are exchanging confidences.' She lowered her face to mine. 'Let me make it quite clear that you will be going back to Stapleford Hall as a maid, and not even that if you make one more moment of trouble.'

I got up leaving my plate behind, smiled sweetly at her, though in reality I would not have minded sinking my teeth in the fleshy part of her upper arm, and I left the room.

I walked into the hallway with great purpose, but after a few steps floundered. There was still nothing to do. I might make my way to the library to read, but this would occasion comment. Ladies, especially royalty, are not meant to be keen readers. By rights I should ring for a small easel and try painting a watercolour, or even start doing some embroidery. But if I did my cover would be blown at once, for I was deeply deficient in both skills.

'Ah, your Highness,' said Robbins, creeping up on me with the typical stealth of his position. 'Chief Inspector Brownly would be honoured if you would spare him a moment of your time when it is convenient.'

'I'll come now,' I said. Robbins's eyebrows almost disappeared into his receding hairline. That I should jump at a civilian's call and one in such a lowly occupation obviously did not fit his idea of how Royalty should behave.

I gave a little impatient wave that was much more in keeping with my supposed character. 'I am bored, Robbins, and I want this matter closed.'

'The Earl would be the first to agree with you

Ma'am,' said Robbins and I got a very slight bow. I had redeemed myself in his eyes.

The chief inspector had been given a draughty room with uncomfortable chairs. It had an aspect that meant it must always lie in the shadows of a copse of trees. The fire was not lit and despite still wearing his coat Brownly was looking a little blue about the gills. Mrs Merion must have orders to make the poor man as uncomfortable as possible, so he would leave as soon as possible. This did not suit my purposes.

I marched into the room and surveyed it with my nose in the air. 'Robbins,' I said, 'send a maid to light the fire. I cannot possible sit in a chilled room. We will also all require tea to keep us warm until the fire does its job.' I stood in front of the chair. 'This chair also requires padding. Either that or have it changed at once!'

The chief inspector, who was in the process of rising to greet me, offered me his hand with a smile. 'Very well said, your highness.'

'And quickly,' I said over my shoulder, 'I have no desire to stand here like an ornamental coat hanger!'

Both chair and tea were quickly fetched, and after a small, very frightened maid had laid and lit a fire, I settled down to be interviewed.

The interview proceeded as one might imagine. Where was I? Did I hear anything? All the very basic stuff to which I could offer no real insight. When the chief inspector asked me about the fight between Richenda and Lady Stapleford I dutifully repeated what she had 'told me in confidence.'

'I am afraid your Highness that I am beginning to come to the conclusion that Lady Stapleford did die of natural causes. If poison is found in her body I may even be looking at self-harm. An aging beauty, widowed, and without financial means to support herself in the life to which she was once accustomed, made to sit through the glorious wedding of a stepdaughter that she does not particularly like. It would be enough to drive some ladies to desperate measures.'

'I do not think Lady Stapleford was like that at all,' I said sharply. I could see the chief inspector had come up with neat scenario to extricate himself from this situation.

'But then you did not really know her, did you, your Highness? A passing acquaintance through her stepdaughter. You had not even met until recently, had you?'

Damn Richenda and her schemes!

'Sir Richard has confided to us that his step-mother had been in poor spirits since the death of his father.'

'And her son?' I asked.

'Regrettably, the doctor feels Mr Bertram Stapleford is not up to answering questions at this time.'

I took an involuntary gasp of breath. 'He will recover, won't he?'

Brownly smiled. 'Dr Threep is confident of a full recovery provided the patient has full rest and quiet.'

Oh, this was all turning out very conveniently for the murderer. 'Did you check her bell was in order?' I asked. I stammered and blushed under

176

his gaze. 'It occurred to me that Lady Stapleford would have called for help.'

'Presuming it was murder,' said Brownly.

'Indeed, if the bell was not working that would prove someone else was involved.'

The chief inspector sat back in his hair and gave me a tired smile. 'It may surprise you to hear that that thought had occurred to this humble policeman. I checked her bell first thing this morning. Robbins assures me it rang in the servants' hall.'

I opened and closed my mouth several times before I could find my voice. 'What if the murderer has fixed it,' I finally offered. Even I knew this sounded weak.

The chief inspector got up and rang the bell. Robbins dutifully appeared. 'Could you confirm to this young lady that the bell in Lady Stapleford's room was indeed working on the night of her demise? And that it was still working when we tried it this morning?'

'I can assure your Highness.' Robbins gave my title emphasis after Brownly's familiarity, 'that all the bells are tested before the guests arrive. The chief inspector this morning with the help of this sergeant' – I finally noticed a small blue uniformed man in the corner with a notepad – 'tested the bell to our mutual satisfaction.'

'Thank you. Robbins.' said Brownly. Once the door had shut behind the butler he said. 'I don't want you to think that we will be making a great deal out of Lady Stapleford's – er–'

'Suicide,' I said starkly, 'that's what you are implying.'

'I am sure I can persuade the corner that it was

death by misadventure.'

'But what if Richenda is telling the truth and her mother had learned something terrible about her fiancée?'

'Can I just stop you there, your Highness,' interrupted Brownly, 'only I'd be very careful about throwing accusations around. People are liable to take offence. Slander is a criminal offence.'

I was so angry I flounced out of the room without bidding the wretched man farewell. All I could think was how Bertram would react to the generally held, but unspoken belief, that his mother had killed herself. I feared it would worsen his condition. Tears pricked at my eyes. It might even prove too much for his constitution. I had to find out what Lady Stapleford knew, but how?

Chapter Twenty-seven

Council of War

I exited only to walk literally into Rory. 'Goodness, Rory, what are you doing standing around in the middle of the corridor.'

'I'm waiting for you Ma'am.' He lowered his voice, 'in public you must call me McLeod.'

'Alright, McLeod,' I said looking up at him and smiling, 'you're looking rather stern. Is anything wrong?'

'I am looking at you in the way a butler must regard a lady with dignity and respect.'

'Don't be silly,' I said looking up and down the corridor and I threw my arms around his neck. These were immediately removed. 'Don't be foolish,' said Rory. 'I have been sent to escort you to Mr Bertram's room. He wishes to know how your police interview went.'

'Is he well enough for that?'

'That is not my place to say, Ma'am,' said Rory and began to lead the way. I stood still watching him retreat for a few moments. I was not sure if he was teasing me about the whole servant and lady business or if he had something on his mind. Rory could be the most eloquent of entertaining speakers, but, as with most men, trying to get him to tell you what he was thinking was akin to opening an oyster with a knife made of jelly. As he reached the end of the corridor I scampered after him. I could find Bertram's room on my own, but only if I went back to the main staircase at the entrance and started from there. Doubtless Rory already knew his way around the complex corridors and passageways of the Court.

I found Bertram sitting up in bed, wearing a garish embroidered jacket and a pale demeanour. 'Where's Merry?' he snapped as Rory and I entered.

'I'm off to find her the now, sir,' said Rory.

'That's not good enough, man! I can't have a woman in here unchaperoned!'

'But she's been your housekeeper,' protested Rory, 'you must often have been a room alone together.'

Bertram reddened. 'Well, whatever happened in the past, it isn't fit now. Would you mind wait-

179

ing outside until Merry is fetched, Euphemia. I am very sorry about this.'

Rory's aspect became more thunderous. I acquiesced at once. Outside Rory refused my assistance in the search for Merry and insisted on bringing me a chair to sit upon. This might sound like a kind gesture, but it was done with a good helping of sulking.

Fortunately, Merry was quickly located and we all entered Bertram's room together.

'How are you feeling?' I asked.

'I'll live,' said Bertram, 'but I feel dammed weak. Blasted doctor says I need plenty of bed rest. Now tell me everything the police said!'

'Is that a good idea?' I queried. 'They were keen you were not to be disturbed due to your in-disposition.'

'Blast and damn it!' spat Bertram. 'I will work myself into far more of a state if I don't know what's going on. Where are you going, man? Sit down. This is a council of war.'

Merry has been serving the Stapleford's far longer than I, but she was sitting twisted her apron in her lap and looking decidedly uncomfortable. Rory was generally glowering. I decided the best course of action to bring us all together was to explain my interview in depth along with the suspicions the chief inspector was now harbouring about suicide.

'That's ridiculous.' Rory was the first to protest. 'There is no way Lady Stapleford would have taken her own life.'

'Of course it is,' said Bertram. 'The man's try-ing to find an easy way out like Euphemia im-

180

plied. The Earl must have been calling in all his connections and they must have made it very clear to Brownly that he needed to be out of here quick.'

Merry opened her mouth to speak, then lowered her head and started twisting her apron again. 'What is it?' I encouraged her. That apron would be in bits in a minute. 'It doesn't make any sense, her killing herself. I did what Euphemia asked and found out about the evening drinks. It's a maid called Lucy what does them and she clearly remembers going into Lady Stapleford's room and handing her drink to her.' Once she started speaking the words didn't stop. 'Lucy said as how she was right scared of going in to the Royalty's room so she thought she'd warm up, as it were, on the Staplefords, only Richenda didn't reply to the knock on her door. Lady Stapleford told her to come in, but then was so fizzingly angry, not with Lucy, from what she says, but obviously in a rare mood, she was throwing clothes and cushions all over the place. Lucy was so scared. She put the cup down and fled. She didn't dare knock on your door afterwards, Euphemia, and just left the cup outside your door even though she knew she'd be on a warning if anything was mentioned to Mrs Merion or Mr Robbins. And I don't reckon how someone who was that angry would be thinking to take their own life, do you? Sounds like she was in such a taking she'd be more likely to do someone else in, begging your pardon Mr Bertram, I mean I know your mother was no killer. I just meant it to show I don't see how she could possibly have harmed herself. It just weren't like her and it

181

weren't like her mood that night.' At this point Merry ran out of air and fell back to twisting her apron. I swatted at her hands to stop her. This made her actually look at what she had been doing. 'Oh Lor', I've ruined it! I'll be in such trouble.'

'I'll buy you a score,' said Bertram. 'I shall get McLeod to ensure this Lucy speaks to the police. It's not definite proof, but it's something in our – and my mother's favour.'

'But if she took the cup herself,' I said, 'how did the poison get into it?'

'It means it must have been added in the kitchen,' said Rory.

'Or while it was on the tray stand,' said Merry. 'They have these little tray rests at just outside the servant's stair entrance onto the bedroom floors. It's so the maids can put down the tray and take the cups individually to the rooms.'

'If it's outside the stair it would be too risky,' I said. 'Whoever did this couldn't be sure they wouldn't be seen.'

'Whoever did this is a risk taker by the nature of the crime,' said Bertram, 'but I agree it would be all too easy to run into the maid. Unless, of course, they were prepared to kill her too, but then no one would think it was suicide.'

'I don't believe the killer cared about that,' said Rory thoughtfully, 'Whoever did this must have put the poison in the cup when it was in the kitchen. At that time of night the staff are either cleaning the dishes, polishing the silver, or waiting on those retiring. A very, very few will be at leisure. The cook would be probably resting in her room.'

'And the trays are left out in the kitchen,' said Merry, 'but the washing and polishing is done elsewhere.'

'So for someone who knew the house it would be possible to sneak in and put poison in the cup, but still risky. The biggest risk would be after the poison was added. If they were caught before they could make up some excuse and abort the task.'

'So this isn't a murder that was planned before we came here,' said Bertram. 'It was something decided on once we arrived at the Court. Which means something changed after we got here.'

'But wait a moment,' I said, 'before we go there. How did the murderer know the right cup to poison? Are they individually labelled?'

'No,' said Merry. 'Lucy said how they are put out for each maid and each maid takes a floor on a wing. For the morning tea, milk and sugar are added at the tray stand, but for the cocoa at night they are all poured from the one jug on the tray. They try to keep it hot for as long as possible.'

'That means the poison was in the cup not the jug,' said Rory.

'Does it?' I asked. 'I never found my drink because it was left outside and Richenda didn't open her door. Merry said she had to remake her drink as it had gone cold.'

Merry raised her hand to her mouth. 'Then it might have been meant to kill all of you,' she said, horrified.

'Well, that would have certainly stopped the wedding,' said Bertram.

'Wait a minute,' said Rory, 'that doesnae make

183

sense. If three ladies had died Earl's residence or no, we would have had police crawling all over the place. It would be a national headline event.'

'Food poisoning,' said Bertram.

Rory shook his head, 'No, I reckon they would have investigated every single pot and pan in the place. The murderer might be reckless, but it would be gey stupid to count on the police passing over three deaths.'

'You're right. McLeod,' said Bertram. 'We're no further on...'

'Oh dear God,' I said under my breath. My face must have been a picture of horror, because despite his mood Rory laid a comforting hand on my shoulder. 'Don't you see,' I said, 'that means the killer couldn't be certain who would get the poisoned cup. He didn't care which one of us died. He simply wanted either Richenda, Lady Stapleford or I to die.'

Chapter Twenty-eight

A Monster Among Us

'But that's monstrous,' said Bertram.

'Unless it was Richenda,' said Merry. 'If she knew one of the cups was poisoned, then leaving it to get cold and having me make another one was a masterstroke.'

'By that token you could equally say it was me,' I said.

'Don't be ridiculous,' said Bertram, 'we know it wasn't you.'

It was a calm, quiet statement of fact, but said with an expression of total trust in his eyes. I felt quite emotional.

'Are we no overlooking the bell?' said Rory. 'Yon polis said it were working. And Robbins said it were tested before the guests arrived.'

'So whoever murdered my mother went into her room and disconnected it after we arrived?'

'Another gey risky manoeuvre,' said Rory.

'Unless,' I said, 'it was someone who'd not be thought to be odd if they were found in her room.'

'You mean like me,' said Merry. 'Cos I didn't do it.'

'We know that,' I said, 'but perhaps another servant or...'

'Richenda,' said Rory.

'Or Richard,' said Bertram.

'Or you,' said Merry, 'but we know you didn't do it.'

Bertram patted Merry's hand making her blush. 'That's sweet of you to say, Merry, but the truth is that although we all trust that each other didn't do this terrible thing it seems as hard to prove that as it to find the real culprit.'

'Could you try asking Richenda what that row was about, Merry?' I asked.

'I'll try,' said Merry, 'but you never know with her what kind of mood she'll be in. One minute it's all have these lovely gloves they'll be good for your day off the next she's throwing a lamp at me.'

'Sounds like she and Tipton are well-suited,' I said.

'What,' said Bertram, 'Baggy's a nasty wee runt I'll give you that, but I've never known him to raise his hand in anger.'

Rory and I exchanged looks. 'That has not been our experience, sir,' he said carefully. 'The maid at Stapleford Hall who didn't fetch him hot enough shaving water certainly bore the brunt of his anger.'

'Really?' said Bertram more intrigued than annoyed at our revelation. 'I always thought the little blighter had no backbone. Mind you, he did propose to Richenda. Not many men would do that.'

Merry had been scowling fiercely. 'If they didn't mind which one of the ladies they killed, what was their reason?'

'Killing any of us would have stopped the wedding,' I said.

'So who wanted that?' asked Rory.

We all looked helplessly at each other. 'You said there was an argument between Tipton and Richard that night. What was that about?'

'It was very late and they were both extremely drunk,' said Bertram. 'They were slurring their words so much I think only they would understand each other. I certainly couldn't.'

'But something must have happened to make Tipton go downstairs again,' I said. 'He looked in on the ladies to say goodnight and proposition Merry. He was in a jolly mood.'

'They only thing I know that happened,' said Merry, 'is the catfight between Richenda and Lady S. I can ask around the servants' hall and see if anyone knows anything else. The maids are

186

all right little gossips.'

'You're all missing the point,' said Rory suddenly, 'the murderer hasn't got what he or she wanted. The wedding is merely postponed.'

'You mean they might try again?' said Merry nervously.

'They already did. With me,' I said.

'What?' said Bertram.

'Someone attacked me in my room,' I said shortly, neither wanting to remember it nor upset Bertram.

'Euphemia, what happened?'

Rory ignored him. 'If that was the same person,' said Rory, 'then it's not Richenda because it was a man who attacked you. But if it is the same person who poisoned Lady Stapleford then we know it's someone desperate.'

'And as the wedding approaches they are only going to get more desperate,' said Bertram.

'Oh, my Gawd,' said Merry. 'That means none of us is safe and those bleeding policemen are being about as useful as a hot water bottle made from a sieve!'

'I think we have to presume it is the same person or someone working with the poisoner. I'm sorry, Bertram, it could be both your half-brother and half-sister.'

'No,' said Bertram, 'I've known them long enough to know that while they may when cornered back each other up, generally their plans don't align.'

'Could they be cornered right now?' asked Rory.

'Richenda is desperate to marry Tipton,' I said. 'I saw the way she accepted his proposal.'

A smile curled Rory's lips, 'It was certainly forceful!'

'Then we're back almost where we started. We need to find out the substance of the arguments.'

'Then that's what we must do,' I said. 'We must also take great care.' The other three nodded solemnly though I knew they were thinking like me how much more care could we take?

Bertram sank back against his pillows, and with one accord we began to edge out of the room.

'We'll get no further here,' said Rory. 'But if we find out anything we'll be back to tell you.' Merry curtsied and muttered something.

Bertram caught me by the arm, 'Wait one moment, Euphemia.'

Merry hesitated by the door.

'She'll only be a minute,' urged Bertram. When she had shut the door behind her he pulled me down gently to sit beside him. 'I've always known you were someone special,' he said, 'but the last few days have shown me that regardless of who your parents might be, you are a lady and must be treated as such. There can be no question of you returning to either my estate or Stapleford Hall as a housekeeper.'

I disentangled his fingers from my sleeve. 'There is no question that I must earn my living to provide for my mother and little brother,' I said firmly, but without anger.

'Something must be done,' said Bertram. 'You belong above stairs. You belong with me.' The effort of saying this sapped the last of his strength. He was quite breathless at the end of his little speech. 'Come,' I said softly, 'rest. We can discuss this when you are well.'

'Damn,' said Bertram. 'I hate being this ill. I hate you seeing me so weak.'

'I have never thought of you as weak,' I said, 'and I don't believe I ever will. Please sleep now before we damage my reputation beyond repair.'

Bertram waved feebly at the door indicating he wouldn't stop me leaving. 'This discussion is not over,' he murmured as I left, but by the time I closed the door he had sunk into a deep slumber.

Outside I found Rory waiting for me. 'This way,' he said brusquely, and more or less shoved me into a side room. It was a dressing boudoir, but from the dust sheets spread around the room, clearly not currently in use. 'I've spoken to Fitzroy,' he said.

'Oh good. Did you persuade him to help us? He wouldn't listen to me.'

'He was only interested in getting me to sign this official secrets document. He said domestic murder didn't interest him.' Rory spoke with an obvious sneer.

I sat down on a covered chair throwing up a little pile of dust. 'Oh dear, I thought he might have listened to you.'

'That man never listened to me,' said Rory sharply, 'but he doesnae know you've been attacked.'

'I expect he would say it was my own fault for getting tangled up in other people's affairs.' I sighed. 'He is a most annoying man. If he wasn't as dangerous I'd give him a piece of my mind.'

Rory knelt down in front of me and took my hands. 'It costs me a lot to say this Euphemia, but if you go to him and tell him what has happened to you he will help. I know he will. I hate to admit it but we need him. You are in too much danger.'

'Why would he help now?' I asked bewildered.

'Have you looked in the mirror?' asked Rory. 'You were always gey bonnie to me, but you're a beautiful woman and a lady without question. There's no man in this house who would not consider it an honour to protect you.'

'Apart from the man that attacked me, you mean,' I said scathingly. 'Get up, Rory. This is silly.'

Rory let go of my hands and stood. He had a mulish look in his face. 'If you won't do what must be done to protect you then I will. I'll not put my pride before your safety,' he said and stormed out leaving me quite speechless.

I dusted myself down as best I could as a fair bit of the dust in the room appeared to now be clinging to me and decided what I needed more than anything was a breath of fresh air to clear my head. A turn in the garden, in full view of the house, would keep me safe and best of all, solitary. As well as trying to solve this mystery, my head was abuzz with the voices and actions of Bertram and Rory. Both of whom I thought were acting far out of character. I caught sight of myself in a mirror as I was about to leave. The woman who looked back at me was a stranger, finely dressed and with a reserved and concerned impression on her face. My hair was different as were my make-up and clothes, but my eyes, the windows of my soul, told a different story; that I was the same inside as I had ever been. I could not help but wonder if either Bertram or Rory knew me at all. My reflection blinked back tears. How could either of them believe that a few fancy clothes would change the real me?

I walked briskly and with purpose down and out into the garden. I was doing my best to avoid the majority of the guests. I knew the longer I was in conversation with a stranger the more chance I had of people discovering who I really was.

I also had a strong feeling there was something I was missing. Not something I had heard, but something I had seen. If I could only work out what this was then I would be several steps closer to understanding what was going on. I needed time and space to think.

It was a fine day. A gardener had been at work somewhere and the scent of freshly mown grass was strong and sweet in the air. Birds called and a faint breeze stirred between the leaves on the trees. Ahead of me I could see a little wooden house, built, I imagined for some long grown up children. The green paint was peeling and spider had spun thick webs across the windows. Still, it was a sweet reminder of happier times. The sounds and smells were so familiar I shut my eyes and imagined myself back in the vicarage garden long before any of this had all begun. In my mind's eye I could see my father, in a battered old straw hat that my mother hated, apologizing to the weeds as he pulled them from the flower beds.

I was so lost in reminiscence that I never heard the footsteps behind me. I had no idea I was not alone until I was firmly taken by the arms and bundled into that sweet little summer house.

Chapter Twenty-nine

A Surprising Appeal for Help

The interior of the summerhouse was dark. A weak light filtered through the cobwebs. This increased substantially when I put my hand through one cluster of webs trying to steady myself. A shaft of sunlight landed on my capturer's face. Electric blue eyes bored into mine. The angry words on my tongue faded. Fear crept over my skin, turning me cold with dread.

'Mr Tipton,' I said in suitably confused tones, 'what is this all about?'

Tipton took a step towards me and I shrunk back against the dirty wooden wall. I could feel my splendid dress catching on splinters. Baggy Tipton held up both his hands. He backed away from me towards the door and shot a bolt home. I took a deep intake of breath and prepared to scream.

'Don't,' said Tipton, 'I don't mean you any harm.'

'It's your normal practice to lock women in summerhouses for their entertainment, is it Mr Tipton? Because I'm not finding this very entertaining.'

'I couldn't think of a way to speak to you alone,' said Tipton. 'When I saw you walking in the garden it seemed too good a chance to miss.'

'You could have simply asked me to meet you?'

'Would you have come?' asked Tipton. I didn't respond. 'I didn't think so. Besides, Rich gets rather jealous, and I didn't want to put her back up before the wedding.'

'What is that you think I can help you with – precisely?'

Tipton sat down on a pile of old stacks, but he kept himself between me and the door. 'I don't know. Can't seem to think straight at the moment. Wedding nerves I expect. If there is going to be a wedding.'

'Has it been called off?'

'Not yet, but I get the distinct impression that Richard doesn't want it to go ahead. Apparently he and Rich are completely at odds. Had a right old ding-dong. And I have no idea why.'

'You argued with Richard on the night of the murder, didn't you? What was that about?'

Tipton frowned. 'Did we? I was very drunk. Someone, a servant, fetched me when Richenda and her stepmother were at it. I got there too late and Richie refused to speak to me. I thought she was giving me the heave-ho, so I went downstairs and got very drunk. Very, very drunk. Everything after that's a bit of a mist. Woke up in me own bed with a thumper of a headache and a mouth like the inside of...' he broke off. 'But that's not the point.'

I waited. Tipton hadn't threatened me yet and he didn't appear violent. I had no intention of provoking him.

'Thing is,' said Tipton rubbing his face in his hands, 'thing is I want you to take back your words. What you told the policeman about Lady S being murdered.'

'I don't believe they think she was,' I said carefully.

'Know me brother, Tip-top? One of the best. Everyone likes him. No, I don't suppose you do. I keep forgetting you're only a servant in that get-up. Looks good on you. Almost a lady and all that.' He rubbed his hands over his face and through his hair. 'Thing is, Tip-top gave me a sort of brotherly warning that one of our guests might be linked to people high up. People who make a habit of knowing stuff. So I need you to tell the police you were wrong.'

'Mr Tipton, I think you overestimate the weight my opinion carries with Chief Inspector Brownly.'

'Damn it,' spat Tipton leaping to his feet and a fist into his palm. 'That's not what I need to hear.' He began to pace up and down the little summer house breathing heavily. Every few steps he slammed his fist into his other hand. Then he start talking very quickly under his breath. I kept very still, but cast my glance about looking for something, anything I could use as a weapon if he came for me. The cobwebby windows were tiny. Even if I smashed one I'd never get through it in this dress and we were far enough away from the main house that no one was likely to hear it.

'I'll do whatever I can do help,' I said. Tipton stopped pacing and threw me an enormous smile. 'I knew you were good stuff,' he said. 'Stepping up to the mark in Richie's hour of need and all that. Thing is, I don't know what you can do. Don't know what any of us can do.'

194

'Why don't you tell me what's worrying you,' I said. 'And I'll do what I can to help.'

At this he launched himself at me, grabbed one of my hands and brought it to his lips. 'Good girl,' he said. 'Good girl. I told Richie you were a good 'un. Damn thing is she's one of those who always takes against the pretty girl and you're a stunner.' He kissed my hand again. I resolved to wash it as soon as I got out of here. If I got out of here. He let me go and began pacing again. 'But it's no good,' he said. 'No good. Can't think of a way out of it. Richard and his bloody deals have drawn too much attention. He's got enemies, you know.' He turned his gaze to me and I saw his eyes were feverishly bright. 'They're out for him.'

'Who?' I asked.

Tipton tapped the side of his nose. 'Better you don't know,' he said, 'but they're there. Waiting in the shadows and they're not going to let this drop. I know they're not. Once we're married it will be all righty-tighty. Related to an Earl and all that. She'll be safe once she's mine.'

'Richenda?' I asked. 'You think someone wants to harm Richenda?'

'No, damn and blast it! Don't you understand? Richenda killed Lady S and I've got to protect her. I've got to be her knight in shining armour and take her away from all this.'

'She told you this?'

'No. No. She's trying to protect me the darling, but I know. She had that fight with her. Stands to reason Lady S must have been trying to stop the wedding. Richie's dead set on marrying me. Determined girl. Doesn't let anything get in her way once she's set her mind to it. Great girl. Fond of her. Have to help. We need to get the policemen out of the house. Maybe we could find a pasty.'

I couldn't see how a picnic was going to help matters. Then light dawned. 'Do you mean patsy?'

'That's what I said,' said Tipton. 'You are taking this seriously, aren't you? You are Richenda's friend, my friend, aren't you?'

'Of course,' I said wondering if I could edge past him to the door. Suddenly he launched himself at me and caught me by the throat. His hand cruelly gripping me. 'Cos if you're not our friend then I'll have to do something about it. I have to protect Richenda. I have to. Nothing. No one will stop me.'

I couldn't speak, but I nodded my agreement as vehemently as I could. He let me go as suddenly as he had attacked. Good girl,' he said in a normal voice. 'Good girl. Here, watch those cobwebs, you'll spoil that lovely frock.'

'Thank you,' I said and forced myself to stay still as he brushed them from my sleeve and skirt.

'What we need to do is find someone else to blame.'

'Good idea,' I said carefully. 'Do you have anyone in mind?' If at this point he had suggested that the moon was made of small lost cats I would have agreed with him.

Tipton waved his hands airily. 'Anyone will do.'

'It might be a good idea for it to be a servant,' I said. 'They are unlikely to have anyone to defend them.'

Tipton approached me and again and pointed

a finger at me for emphasis. 'Excellent idea. Excellent. That's the kind of thinking I need.'

'Merry knows all the servants,' I said. 'I could get her to tell me about them. You know how she loves to gossip and she wouldn't have any idea why. Then I could pick someone out and let you know.'

Tipton put his head on one side. 'She wouldn't know why we were doing it? I've always had a bit of a soft spot for Merry and I'd hate to have to...' This was said in a tone of genuine regret as if we were debating whether or not to invite Merry to a tea party. His casualness frightened me. I kept thinking I must have misunderstood.

'I promise she'd have no idea,' I said and crossed my heart.

'Good-ho,' said Tipton. 'I knew I did the right thing coming to you.' He unbolted the door and flung it open. 'Great little chat. I'll catch up with you later when you've got the dirt. Good girl.'

I walked to the door. He didn't move. I walked head high out into the garden. As soon as I rounded a corner in the path and was out of sight I lifted at my skirts and ran as fast as I could for the house.

Chapter Thirty

Something Wicked This Way Comes

I sprinted past an alarmed Robbins and made straight for my room. Once I was there I locked the door and popped the key down my neckline. Then I threw myself onto the bed and hugged a pillow to my face to muffle my sobs. I had every intention of seeking help, but not until I was once again mistress of my emotions.

Robbins must have reported my disgraceful entry to Merry because it wasn't long before she was knocking at my door. I let her in. She took in the tears on my face and my tattered dress and drew all the wrong conclusions. I ended up explaining the whole story to her, in I admit less than my usual concise manner, and Merry became immediately practical. Being Royalty I had been given a room with an attached bathing chamber. She ran me a bath full of bubbles, more or less pushed me into it, after helping remove my dress, told me to have a good soak and she would arrange for cakes and tea in my room when I was out.

An hour later I sat down at a little table in my room and Merry poured me tea. She also helped herself to a small, iced cake. She bit into it greedily and icing stuck to her nose. 'They don't feed the staff here as well as Mrs Deighton does,' she said

198

in self-defence.

It suddenly struck me as funny that we were sitting down eating afternoon tea and it was almost time for the dinner dressing gong. What's more, I was pretending to be a housekeeper pretending to be a minor foreign Royal, when in reality I was an Earl's granddaughter whose grandfather was about to sit down to dinner on the floor below; he had even sat beside me without knowing who I was. Moreover, the man I suspected of being a killer, and of doing away with Mrs Wilson and possibly Miss Wilton too, had just asked me to help him find a patsy for the girl he wanted to marry, who he was sure had killed her stepmother. It was all too ridiculous. I laughed so hard tears ran down my cheeks. I doubled up with laughter, only pausing to draw breath before I went into whoops again. Before I had only read of going into whoops, but now I was actually doing it.

The door flew open. Richenda stormed in. 'What the hell is that noise?'

Merry jumped to her feet, thrusting the remains of the cake behind her back. The sight of Richenda, nostrils flaring and looking more like a warhorse than ever, was too much. I fell off my seat.

'Cor blimey, she's lost it,' said Suzette, peering over Richenda's shoulder. 'I told the mistress she was an odd one, but it's all been too much for the little blighter.'

The sight of Suzette's pinched face, she looked as if she had been crudely made out of not enough clay, sobered me dramatically. I sat up,

199

wiped away my tears with the back of my hands. 'You!' I said. 'Your face. I remember that look. You looked ... you looked,' but the memory wouldn't come back fully.

'Very sad, milady,' said Suzette. 'I'm sure her maid can contain her. It's time for me to dress you for dinner.'

Richenda gave me a pitying look. 'Don't let her come down tonight, Merry. I'll say she is indisposed.'

I stood up, drawing my dressing gown around me in what I hoped was a regal manner, and said, 'It is not your place to order me around, Richenda.'

'How dare you?' screamed Richenda. 'How dare you address me like this!'

'Not two hours ago I was with your beloved in the summer house,' I said suddenly calm as ice, 'and he told me that you murdered Lady Stapleford.'

'What!' cried Richenda. 'Tippy would never say anything like that!'

'He asked me to help him find someone to fit up for the crime.'

Richenda went deathly pale. 'He can't ... he can't ... but that would mean... Oh my God,' she cried and fled from the room. Suzette followed at once, slamming the door.

'I reckon she thought Tippy had done it, don't you?' said Merry.

'Yes,' I said slowly. 'I think she did and the two idiots have been trying to protect each other.'

'Well, your hysterics were good for something after all.'

'If we're right,' I said, 'it means we need to rethink what we know about the crime. We've just lost our two main suspects.'

'Look,' said Merry, 'if you're feeling okay then I reckon you should go down to dinner. It might be that...'

'Something is revealed over the oysters?' I said, feeling a bubble of mirth rising within me again.

'Now, stop that at once,' said Merry. 'I'm going to go below stairs and tell Rory about your latest adventure and if that doesn't wipe the smile off your face you ain't got no sense. He's going to be downright furious with Tipton and you!'

'It wasn't my fault!'

'You keep swanning off on your own and you keep getting pounced on. See any connection? 'Cos if you don't I'm sure Rory will.'

'I am definitely going to go hide among the Earls,' I said. 'Help me dress, Merry.'

As she finished my hair Merry said, 'It's nice Tipton liked me, isn't it?'

'Oh yes,' I responded, 'he said he'd actually regret killing you.'

Merry froze for minute, not in shock as I first thought, but in thought, 'He's quite mad, isn't he? I mean really mad. Do you think we should stop this wedding?'

'I think someone already has that well in hand,' I said. 'We just need to find out who and why.'

'Same old, same old,' muttered Merry as she hustled me through the door. 'Now don't you go getting locked in with anyone else! No wandering off on your own!'

The effect of these strictures was to make me

feel like a six year old playing dress up at an adults' party. People were gathering in the hall for drinks before dinner. From the top of the staircase I could see all the original faces I had seen when I first arrived, but this time voices did not echo around the chamber. Instead the conversation was more of a dull buzz. Many of the drinkers cast glances over their shoulders every third or fourth sip as if they expected an assassin to creep up on them from behind.

The Earls and the Countess stood alone to one side. All three countenances reflected a dismay and distrust of the situation before them. Richenda sat in one of the few grand chairs. Tipton hovered attentively at her side. From time to time the two regarded each other in a way that extinguished my already small appetite. While I dressed they had clearly forgiven each other of all suspicions. I had no more time to pick out anyone I had reached the bottom stair.

Immediately my arm was taken. 'I have been hearing about your unfortunate times,' said Fitzroy/Milford. 'Come through this way and I will get you a proper drink.'

I instinctively stiffened. 'Don't worry,' said Fitzroy, 'not only will everyone see you leave with me, but I am probably – no definitely – the safest person you could be with right now.'

I did not go with him because of this argument, but rather because I feared making that total social faux par, causing a scene. As I accompanied him into one of the side chambers which proved to be yet another small study I reflected that if Fitzroy wanted me dead he would undoubtedly accomplish it more discreetly.

He poured and handed me a small Scotch with instructions to sip it slowly. 'You don't need to tell me you're not used to that kind of drink,' he said.

'Not exactly a lady's tipple,' I replied, trying to suppress a shudder as the strong liquor hit my stomach. 'Now what is it I can do for you?'

Fitzroy pulled forward a couple of chairs and indicated I should sit. He waited for me to sit first in the manner one would have done with a real lady, but then he knew who I was.

'I don't have all the facts,' he admitted much to my surprise, 'but I am hearing alarming rumours about the situations you have recently found yourself in. I brought you through here to advise you to leave the Court. I can arrange for a suitably impressive carriage to pick you up.'

'Thank you,' I said sincerely. 'I know it is unlike you to engage yourself in such minor matters.'

Fitzroy gave a little snort of laughter. 'Touché,' he said.

'I didn't mean to be rude,' I said struggling for the right words, 'I meant that I understand that you are here to work and that you mustn't compromise your identity.'

He nodded. 'Correct. I wouldn't interfere unless I felt you to be real danger.'

'Even that surprises me,' I said candidly.

A very faint blush stole into his cheeks. 'You have been useful to us and I would like you to remain alive, so you can be useful again.'

I smiled with genuine appreciation and he broke off his gaze at me. 'I cannot tell you how much I appreciate your offer,' I said, 'but the truth is I have nowhere to go but Stapleford Hall and I do not think my employers would thank me for abandoning them.'

'Those damn bloody people!' said Fitzroy. 'Why the hell did you have to go and work there!'

'They were the only people who would accept me without a reference.'

'Which should have told you something!'

'It told me,' I said coldly, though I boiling with fury inside, 'that I might have a chance of preventing my mother and younger brother from falling into destitution. My mother wrote repeatedly to my grandfather over the years and he never replied. Not even when he knew father was dead and we were homeless would he interest himself in us.'

'Man's a stupid oaf,' said Fitzroy. 'I could talk to him for you.'

'You'd do that?' I said amazement diluting my anger.

'You have a remarkable ability to make me want to do things that I would normally not contemplate for anyone else.'

'Good heavens,' I said ironically, 'is this a declaration of affection, Mr Fitzroy?'

'Milford,' he corrected automatically. 'No, I don't have time for romance in my business, but you remind me of myself. Or how I was when I first entered the service. You're a survivor. You adapt to what life throws at you. It's a skill that is all too rare. I appreciate your determination to seek justice even when the rules don't seem to allow it ever to be found. What worries me is that you are untrained and unfit for the situations you blindly thrust yourself into.'

'Tipton and Richenda have accidently alibied each other,' I said. I succeeded in diverting him.

'Really. And you believe them?'

'Tipton asked me to find someone to take the fall for Richenda and when Richenda learned Tipton was trying to do this she immediately mended her argument with him.'

'So she thought he had done it,' said Fitzroy and gave a low whistle. 'I must admit I didn't see that coming. This is a far greater tangle than I had imagined. Whoever is behind this all is playing their hand with great skill.'

'I agree,' I said. 'He or she is a formidable opponent.'

His face split into a grin. 'I'm not going to get you to leave this alone, am I?'

'No,' I said. 'But I do appreciate the offer. Very much.'

'I'll watch your back as much as I can,' said Fitzroy, 'but I cannot promise to be on hand when the pieces start falling. You cannot rely on me.'

I stood up and held out my hand. 'Oh, Mr Fitzroy,' I said, 'I would never do that.'

Chapter Thirty-one

Not Going Into the Garden

Fitzroy left the room before me and I chose to wait for a few moments before following him. He left the door slightly ajar, so I could hear the hum of pre-dinner conversation. I slipped out and went to stand at the back of the hall. I took a drink from a servant for form's sake, but only let it wet my lips. I had a feeling that I would need to keep my wits very sharp from now. Fitzroy's incredible offer only confirmed to me there games afoot that I knew little about.

Two male guests whose faces I recognised from the first night, but who had not been introduced to me were weaving their way across the hall. They had undoubtedly tried to take the edge of all events by investing heavily in the joys of Bacchus. I watched their progress with some little enjoyment when one of them caught my eye-line, nudged his partner, who attempted to bend his head to hear what his friend was saying and almost took his eye out on the cocktail stick in his bizarre drink. They stumbled together for a moment then like some kind of hideous four legged monster they adjusted course and made straight for me. It didn't take me more than a moment to understand that alcohol had lessened their inhibitions for approaching a member of minor royalty and they were headed straight for me.

I did the only thing I could think of and slipped out into the garden. In my head I could hear Merry's voice cautioning me about separating from the masses, but the thought of dealing with two drunken upper-class twits, who might at any moment throw up on my shoes was too much to bear. Also they were of an age where they might know some of the real Princess's friends and, drunk or not, it would be quickly clear that I had idea what Button-Nose or Squiffy had done last summer. In fact, with the nicknames these people insisted on giving each other I could never be sure if they were referring to each other, their pets or their horses.

I was not in a sociable mood. Frankly, I was fed up with this set, and if Rory had appeared from behind a tree and suggested we elope at that moment I would happily have gone with him. Moreover I would have made it a condition of our nuptials that we would both leave service and set up in a profession were we were more likely to meet decent people who weren't forever trying to kill each other. A tobacconist's seemed like a good choice.

Once I was in the garden I slipped behind a tree and crept like some weirdly sparkly creature from tree to tree until I was a little way from the house, but not without hailing distance. I would still be able to hear the dinner gong and join the crowd as they headed off to feed. Because goodness knows come hell or high water the upper class must dress for dinner and dine, dine, dine! My father's voice now joined Merry's warning voice in my head. He berated me gently for thinking so little of my fellow creatures who were after all made in God's image. This made me thankful my father was not present to hear my answers to such strictures.

I found a particularly broad tree and smooth barked tree (I had to watch my dress) and leaned back. I started to count my blessings as my father had taught me to do when I was in a vile mood. I couldn't remember when I had been quite so angry, but as I mentally listed the people I had who cared about me, the kindnesses I had been shown, I felt unwanted emotion welling up inside me. After all that had happened it made sense that only my anger was keeping me from breaking down and weeping.

Whether I would have given in to my weaker emotions and whether or not I would have fled the Court down the lane and into a new life will never be known for at that moment I had the hair-raising sensation that I was not alone. Without thinking I hunched down at the foot of the tree as if I might be mistaken for a bush. (My only excuse for this foolishness is that by this point in our adventure I was extremely stressed as I hope you may realise.)

Fortunately the two people who had joined me in the garden were far too busy whispering heatedly from one to another. They were also taking a strange, haphazard route though the gardens and I realised they were attempting to hide from the sight of the guests in the Hall. This made me feel a little easier. Here were two people certainly not hunting me, but in fear of being hunted themselves. I moved sideways into an actual bush and attempted to attain some sort of still squatting position. A shoot tickled the inside of my ear. I then became more worried about the thought that a spider or ladybird might be wandering along this shoot and into said orifice. If I moved I would give myself away. I willed the pair to hurry past.

As they grew nearer I forgot about the shoot and possible invasion of my ear, Tipton walked side by side with Suzette. Their heads were close and they were whispering furiously, each speaking over the other. I could not make out what they were arguing about, but then they stopped right in front of me. I held my breath, but they were far too busy negotiating to notice me in my bush.

'I've kept me mouth shut,' said Suzette. 'But your good lady hasn't offered me no job and a girl's got to look after herself in this world.'

'I do see that,' said Tipton.

'I've come a long way as you well know,' said Suzette, 'and I have no intention of going back.'

'You've done well. Extremely well. And Lady S had no idea?'

'Nope. None whatsoever. Your girlfriend knew me though. Took her a while, but she figured it out. Very good about it she was. I'll say that for her, but as I said she ain't offered me no job and with the other one gone I'm on me uppers.'

'And we can't have that,' said Tipton. He took something out of his coat and passed it to Suzette, who immediately stuffed it down her bodice. 'It's on account,' he said. 'I won't get my hands on the money until after the wedding.'

'And the job?' asked Suzette.

'I know you think you've got me here,' said Tipton, 'but a fellow doesn't get to where I am without learning a thing or two. We may be able to come to a financial arrangement, but I think having you on my household staff might be just a bit too dangerous, don't you?'

Suzette's jawline clenched. 'If that's the way you want to play it then I want more before the wedding.'

'My dear girl,' said Tipton, 'you can ruin me at any moment of your choosing. Wouldn't it make sense to let me get my hands on the dosh?'

Suzette lent forward and poked Tipton in the chest with one bony finger. 'I've got brothers,' she said. 'Brothers who know where I am and what I'm doing. If anything happens to me then they'll find you and your new missus.'

Tipton backed away. 'Won't harm a hair on your charming head,' he said. 'Word of a gentleman.'

'Well, as long as we understand each other.'

'I think we do,' said Tipton, nervously fingering his collar.

'And just so you know, I always carry a shank on me. Me brother Bertie learned me how to use it too.'

'I remember,' said Tipton. 'Now, I have to get back to the house before I'm missed.'

'Word of advice,' said Suzette, 'that girl masquerading for you, that Eulogy or whatever. You need to watch her.'

Tipton gave her broad smile. 'All in hand,' he said. He tipped an imaginary hat to her and

210

made his way quickly back towards the house. Suzette pulled the packet out of her bodice and began to count her cash. 'Bleeding, tight fisted little sod,' she said when she had finished and stalked off towards the servants' entrance.

I waited far longer than was necessary then gradually stood up. I brushed myself down as best I could and pulled leaves from my hair. I was happy to find both my ears had no unwanted guests. The dinner gong sounded. I knew I would be missed if I went to my room to tidy, so I lifted my chin and prepared to tell anyone who questioned me that I had a deep love of nature and views.

How Merry would laugh if she could hear me.

Chapter Thirty-two

The Earl is Relieved

The only good thing that could be said about dinner was that the food was delicious. Our seating plan had reverted to that of the first night so I sat between my grandfather and Renard Layfette. My grandfather's attention was taken up by the lady on his other side. He did attempt to break this off and chat to me, but my monosyllabic answers discouraged him.

I was thinking over what I had seen in the garden. How could Tipton know Suzette? Why was she blackmailing him, and what relevance, if

211

any, did have it to the murder? Tipton had been very convincing about wishing to save Richenda from the noose. He might have a variable and even violent temperament and be an obnoxious little squirt, but I didn't think he had the intelligence to lie to me – at least not so long and complicated a lie about fearing for Richenda. I had no idea if he loved her, but I felt sure he felt a deep affection for her money. Halfway through my pigeon squab I decided that Suzette must know something about Tipton's previous love affairs. It was what the police might call a diversion.

Having satisfied myself on this point I began to mentally think over possible suspects. Renard Layfette chose that moment to almost choke on a fish bone. I turned to him in concern, but he was already placing the offending article discreetly in his folded napkin.

'Are you quite well?' I asked.

He gave a very Gallic shrug. 'As I said before, the chef is not French. One take one's life in one's hands eating English food.'

'I have heard rumours that you and Lady Stapleford were not as good friends as you led me to believe before.' The words were out of my mouth before I could consider what I was saying.

'Ah, the refreshing bluntness of the continent,' said Renard. 'None of the English mimsy-whimsy tiptoeing around. Now if only the Earl would take a leaf from your book and tell the police to, er, *bugger off*, we could all get back to normal.'

I waited.

Another shrug followed. This time so big I

thought he was in danger of losing his jacket. 'Heh,' he said. 'The truth is she hated me with a loathing quite intense. I was a wild youth – a sign of spirit I think, but my father did not agree. He banished me and I was forced to make my own way in the world.'

'You told the police you knew Lady Stapleford well and that she had an allergy to oysters.'

'The Earl he said he would smooth things over for me if I did him this tiny favour. I did not see the harm. She was a dislikeable woman. No doubt she did eat something that disagreed with her. There was no need for such a fuss. She was a widow without money. A person of no account.'

This was said without heat or rancour. 'Is your father still alive? Did you hope to be reunited?' I asked trying to think of the most favourable way to take his confession.

'No. No. He is long dead. And I have no need of money. I made a lot, you see, running gambling rooms on the continent. One of the reasons your good Lady Stapleford could not stand me was I, the degenerate one, made far more of a success of my life than her.'

'Where you two once close?'

Renard laughed. 'There might have been affection in the past on her side, but I had no money. And as for me, I was not, er, interested in what she could offer.' He patted my hand. 'I am sorry, *cherie*, there is no tragedy of grand passion for you to uncover. I thought only to help the Earl out in return for an entrée into higher circles. My life has been entertaining, but I miss,' he spread his hands out, 'gatherings such as this.'

I could not repress a shudder. Renard laughed again. 'It is all too much for the nerves of a gentle one such as yourself. You should marry. There are plenty of young men here who would be happy to be wed to a rich, beautiful, royal woman like yourself. Get a ring on your finger then you can really begin to live your life.' He raised an eyebrow. 'You understand me?'

I was spared having to answer this as the Earl got to his feet and tapped loudly on the side of his glass.

'Ladies and gentlemen, I am now able to announce that Lady Stapleford will be laid to rest in our family chapel tomorrow. I am happy to say Chief Inspector Brownly tells me he is confident of closing the case very shortly. After discussion with all family members and the local vicar we have concluded that Lady Stapleford would not have wished the wedding to be postponed. Therefore two days after the funeral the wedding will take place. The police have asked you to remain here until tomorrow evening, and the Countess and I would like to invite you to extend your stay to include the wedding. It will now be a much smaller affair after the recent tragic events and no other family members will be joining us. I do hope you consent to stay and to enjoy what promises to be a very happy day. Can I ask you now to lift your glasses in a toast to our brave bride and groom who have endured so much!'

Everyone except Richenda and Tipton stood. 'To the bride and groom!' Richenda blushed, if not prettily then appropriately, and Tipton grinned from ear to ear. He took her hand and kissed it.

The Earl had cleverly timed his speech to come before dessert, so when an enormous meringue construction with fruits and sauce was set before each diner the mood set was brighter than it had been for days. The waiters then bustled about with a very good dessert wine. Even the long windows of the dining room were thrown open to catch the last of the summer evening. There was a strong feeling of relief in the room that a corner had been turned and everything would now be all right.

The confectionary in front of me turned my stomach and I sent the wine waiter away. 'Do they know who the killer is then?' I said thinking out loud.

Renard answered me. 'Perhaps they have someone. It would be strange to warn us if they thought it was one of us. I expect it is simply being – how do you say – hushed up. Quite right!'

Bertram sat several seats away from me and across the table. I was glad to see him up and about. His face had lost its deathly pallor, but his lips were pressed together in a thin line. He too avoided eating the dessert.

We broke shortly after that with the Countess leading the ladies to the withdrawing room. I had earned a reputation for not joining the throng. Whether it was assumed I was shy or thought myself above their company I had no idea. I wanted to talk to Bertram. I could not imagine that he had easily consented to have his mother laid to rest here. I decided to withdraw to the music room. The doors between the music room and the main library room were open. On the opposite side of the room the doors to the billiard room had also been thrown open, so the three great rooms interconnected. The Drawing room was on the other side of the corridor and it was to the library side I assumed that the men often retreated after dinner. Opening the doors between the three rooms must be meant to encourage them to mingle and even allow the ladies licence to cross the hall and join them. A baby grand stood in the corner of the music room. It was angled in such a way that the player could see into both other rooms, but remained partly obscured by some sort of potted foliage.

I seated myself at the piano, raised the lid and laid my fingers on the smooth, cold keys. As my mother is an expert at the piano I can play. I do not do it with enjoyment, but rather out of duty. I doubt I give much pleasure to any who hear me. Rather than draw attention to my presence I decided to leave the piano open, so that if anyone else did enter then I could simply say I was pondering what to play and if absolutely necessary could do so. My fingers were long out of practice, so I determined to leave this as a last resort. Across the hall I could hear the ladies chatting and even laughing. The pall that had laid across this house party had lifted without a doubt. I felt more uneasy than ever?

Chapter Thirty-three

Behind a Pot-plant with the Hon. Bertram

The gentlemen lingered long enough over their port for it to become decidedly chilly. Smelling the evening summer flowers is nice, but not at the cost of turning blue at the edges. If Bertram had kept up with the circuits of port he must be well inebriated now. I was in the point of giving up and retreating to my room and the fire therein when the man himself entered the hallway. I played a quick arpeggio to attract his attention and then beckoned him into the room.

Bertram sat down next to me on the piano stool. I don't know if he had drunk too much port to be able to judge the distance, but he sat very close to me. Not touching, but I could feel his body heat through my thin dress. 'Always full of surprises,' he said. 'I had no idea you could play.'

'I don't play very well,' I replied, 'but I thought this was the easiest way to speak to you. Are you content with how things are going?'

'And so careful in your use of language. Tipton asked me earlier if I was happy with what was going on and I damn near punched him. The only thing that stopped me was the knowledge I'd be as likely to severely injure myself with this dicky heart of mine as damage that pipsqueak.'

'He shut me in the Summer House with him.'

'He what?' interrupted Bertram, half rising from his seat.

I caught his arm. 'He did me no harm. Instead he wanted me to help him find someone to take the fall for your mother's murder. He was convinced it was Richenda.'

Bertram sat back down. 'Richenda?'

'But when I told Richenda this, and before you say I should have talked to you first let me say there were mitigating circumstances, she was relieved. She'd been acting so strangely because she thought Tipton had done the murder.'

Bertram ran his hand through his hair. 'Good grief, so it was neither of them?'

'If either of them had simply denied it I wouldn't have believed them, but they are both so obviously relieved and I don't think either of them is that good an actor.'

'No,' said Bertram. 'Richenda wears her heart on her sleeve and Tipton hasn't the brains.'

'He was very odd when he was with me. Ranting and confused. He didn't seem right.'

'When has he ever?' said Bertram.

'No, but...'

'This means we are stuck with the theory that someone poisoned one of the cups and didn't care who it killed as long as it was one of you three. That's madness.'

'No, I am not discussing this ANY further!' Tipton's voice loud and angry cut across ours. He crossed the hall and went into the library. Following close on his heels came Richard Stapleford. He face was flushed red with wine and his hands were held by his side clenched into two meaty fists. He followed Tipton into the library and closed the doors to the hall. As one Bertram and I leaned back behind the potted plant, so we could see through the adjoining door and hopefully remain unseen. The view was impeded, but I could make out both men striding around the room. Tipton kept moving away from Richard.

'We can debate this later,' said Tipton.

'You've made one too many remarks about Richenda's money,' said Richard. 'I want to know what you're planning.'

'I have done nothing of the sort,' protested Tipton.

'You never do remember what you say when you're drunk, Baggy. You've always been that way.'

'Stop using that ridiculous nickname,' said Tipton, 'by God I'll plant you one right in the middle of your fat face.'

'The worm is turning,' whispered Bertram in my ear.

'I am not your lackey. I'm not your fag. You can do your own dirty work from now on.'

'Keep your voice down,' said Richard. 'This is a family matter.'

'Yes, it is,' said Tipton, 'and you'd be well to remember that. All your sister is doing is handing over her bank shares to me. It's not appropriate for her to give you her proxy vote when she has a husband.'

'Do you mean to challenge me for the bank?' Richard's face was now a deep violet and I seriously wondered if his heart would burst. However, he kept his voice low.

'That's rather up to you,' said Tipton. 'As you said, it's all in the family now. What's the difference between Richenda holding the votes or me? Except that I don't look like some kind of accessory she's picked up.'

'You might as well be, you're so small,' said Richard.

'Look Richard,' said Tipton, and his voice was that of a man talking to an angry child, 'you wanted me to marry Richenda because frankly she wasn't getting any other offers and you wanted someone who would put the right word in her ear when it was necessary. I will do that. This is the best outcome for all of us.'

'The morning after you got engaged, Richenda started muttering about how she would no longer be under my thumb. And now the wedding's almost upon us, she has told me plainly that she is going to use you to challenge me for control of the bank. The phrase she used was this is only the beginning.' I need to know if you've got her in hand or worse if you're working with her?'

'Oh come on, Richard,' said Tipton, 'you know men will agree to anything before the marriage contract is signed.'

'The question, is what will you do once you are officially family?' said Richard.

'Might I point out it's a little late for this discussion,' said Tipton. 'Besides I think we both know each other well enough not to do anything foolish. Our fortunes are linked in so many ways.'

'He sounds perfectly sane to me,' whispered Bertram. 'Didn't think he had that much backbone in him.'

'He thinks he's home and dry,' I said. 'Look at Richard's face. He is not happy. Your half-brother bothers me when he's not happy.'

Tipton and Richard had ended their discussion and were now making their way across to the Drawing room with little sign of their previous animosity.

'Richard has done some bad things, I grant you,' said Bertram, 'but it's not like he murders people for a hobby.'

'Are you sure?' I said. 'I have two remaining suspects for your mother's murder and he is one. We've just heard him say they've been arguing over what will happen with the bank shares for some weeks. The death of any of the three of us would have been thought enough to stop the wedding.'

'Whoever else he dislikes, Richard has a soft spot for Richenda. She's his twin.'

'Yes, but she's never challenged him before.'

'Nonsense,' said Bertram. 'Who's your other suspect.'

'Renard Layfette.'

'Renard? He wouldn't hurt a fly, unless you count gossiping it to death.'

'But your mother wouldn't even have his name mentioned in his presence and I know he is keen to get back into English society.'

'My mother wouldn't have made much difference to that. She's not the reason he was ostracised.'

'Renard said your mother once even fancied herself in love with him,' I said stretching a point. To my amazement Bertram started to laugh.

'Goodness, that would have been difficult for her.'

'Renard said he didn't want what she was offering. What did he mean?'

Bertram wiped a tear from his eye. 'Have you heard the term "men who play backgammon"?' he asked.

'What do games have to do with this?'

'Oh dear,' said Bertram, blushing. 'Euphemia, there are some men who don't like the company of women.'

'Yes,' I said, 'what about that?'

Bertram took a deep breath, 'I mean ... they prefer men romantically!'

I thought about this for several minutes. 'But how can that even *work?*'

'Good Lord, Euphemia, that's not the sort of question you should be asking me – or anyone. Just accept that my mother's death would have made no impact on Renard's situation.'

'But then the only suspect is Richard and you won't allow that.'

'Perhaps the police have come up with something else. I don't know about you, but I don't know half the people here.'

'But what if they say it's death by misadventure.'

'Then I will accept that,' said Bertram. 'I cannot see any way we can unravel this tangle. It may indeed me that Mama did react to something she ate. It may seem unfeeling of me, but I want to live my life looking forward. Mama adored me in her own way and I know she would want me to carry on.'

'But what about justice!' I protested.

'Euphemia, haven't you realised by now there is very little justice in this world?'

'That's no reason to give up!'

He took my hand in his and stroked his index finger across my palm. 'I admire your dedication and your integrity, but sometimes it is necessary to concede the fight in order to win the war.'

'I don't agree. I will make a point of speaking to Chief Inspector Brownly tomorrow and telling him all I know.'

'That is your choice,' said Bertram, 'but be careful you do not get yourself into a situation you cannot get out of. Now, I am tired. I am retiring. I suggest you do the same. Perhaps the police will be able to explain things fully in the morning.'

He did look tired. There were shadows under his eyes and his shoulders slumped. Bertram was clearly still not fit and I saw no point in forcing an argument he was determined to deflect. I could have railed at him about his sense of justice, but I knew what it was like to lose a beloved parent and now Bertram had lost both his parents in a short space of time. Instead of thinking his morals were weak, I determined to think of him as one battered and bruised by recent misadventures. I felt sure the quick-blooded, impassioned man I had once known would be back on form when he had recovered. Perhaps even after a decent night's sleep. So I wished him well and retired for all early night myself.

I told Merry the little I had learned. She suggested we tackle Suzette together the next day, but I told her I'd rather not bother. I reminded her that we were not the police and did not need to tackle everything. I said I could not see how it could possibly be relevant to what had occurred.

And in saying this I made one of the biggest mistakes of my life. A mistake I will regret until my dying day.

Chapter Thirty-four

Secrets Will Out

I awoke to find the sunlight trying to creep through my heavy curtains. I sat up and immediately huddled back under the blankets. No one had lit the fire in my room yet. No one had drawn the curtains. I am able to draw my own curtains, but I draw the line at laying my own fire. I threw the covers back and rushed for my dressing gown. Once I had tied myself firmly into this I gave the bell a hearty tug. Then I took the topmost cover off the bed and wrapped myself up in a seat that was pointedly by the fire. No one came.

Sunlight flooded the room and pushed the temperature up slightly. I could no longer see my breath in front of my eyes. However, now I was beset with chills of another kind. My imagination, which has always been healthier than my mother would wish, began suggesting all kinds of terrors. I rang the bell again. Still nothing. By this point I had become convinced that some serial madman had run through the house murdering people in their sleep and for some unaccountable reason had overlooked me. Fitzroy seemed to like me. Perhaps he had chosen to let me live.

I folded back the blanket and stood up. This is arrant nonsense, I told myself. I may have seen more deaths than is proper for a young woman, and I may have inadvertently become caught up in a suspicious number of murder cases, but that is no reason to think that the world has descended into chaos. It is far more likely, I told myself, that the aging Robbins took the key to the servants' block to bed within after having one too many tipples and has overslept or has misplaced the key.

But, said my rational mind which was meant to be working to calm me, if that was the case wouldn't someone else have a key – like the house-keeper or the Countess. I began to mentally scold myself before I realised that this form of internal communication was surely a road to madness and the very best thing I could do was go out and see what was happening.

I opened my wardrobe. The dresses hung there, beautiful and complicated. I could possibly scramble into one, but I would have to leave parts undone. I could try and cover these with a shawl, but not knowing what I would find I wanted to keep my hands free.

This is why at 10 a.m. on the morning of Lady Stapleford's funeral, I found myself creeping along the corridors in my night clothes. I went to Richenda's room first. I scratched at the door in the way a lady might, but receiving no answer I gave it a hard knock. The door swung open beneath my hand.

If I hadn't had the privilege of tidying her rooms

at Stapleford Hall, I might have thought the room had been ransacked. She was the messiest woman I had ever met. Clothing and periodicals were strewn across the room. A large amount of powder lay spilt across the dressing table. I noted her bed had been slept in, so whatever had happened she had awoken or been awoken. I did not see any blood or obvious signs of a fight, so I thought there was no point searching the room further. All I would accomplish would be getting the smell of her clothing on me. Richenda had a terrible habit of not allowing anyone to clean her clothes as frequently as they should be. I had cause to remember this as she had once shut me in a wardrobe with her favourite frocks.

The only other room on my corridor was Lady Stapleford's. I had no intention of trying that. Anyone in that room would be either up to no good or making an unearthly appearance, and without breakfast I was not up to facing either.

I returned to my room and swapped my slippers for stronger shoes. I brushed my hair quickly and pinned it back simply. I had no choice, but to attempt to get into the simplest gown. Fortunately Merry had found me one for the funeral that was both black and unfussy. In the mirror I saw someone who looked very like Euphemia the housekeeper rather than the Princess I was pretending to be. My reflection showed signs of worry and her hair had tendrils already curling loose from their moorings, but at least I was now fit to be seen in the public areas of the house – and in particular the quarter that houses both the bedrooms of Bertram and Fitzroy. I wanted to go to Rory, but I knew that nothing short of the collapse of the British Empire itself would explain a Princess entering the servants' quarters.

I crept out of my room and long the corridor leading from the main staircase. From over the banisters I could see a number of policemen standing in the great hall below. Chief Inspector Brownly strode across the hallway as I was watching. He did not look up. His shoulders were set well back and he walked with confidence. From his carriage I surmised he felt he had solved the mystery, but it was more than satisfaction I saw in his movement. He moved very differently than the man who had been forced to be so deferential to the Earl.

You may think I am making too much of this, but in truth servants learn to tell a lot about those they serve by the attitudes by which they carry themselves. In a large gathering the upper classes are no different than a pack of dogs; they will always respect the leader of the pack. Brownly was no longer metaphorically showing his belly. He was very much the man in charge.

Could he have arrested Richenda? That would explain her absence, but I had seen her all too believable relief when she learned that Tipton had not been the culprit. I did not hold the illusion that the two of them loved each other, but I knew they had made a pact that would serve them both well. Tipton would gain money and Richenda status. Had they murdered Lady Stapleford together? But what would be the point?

I crossed the gallery into the area where the single men had been put. I moved as silently as I

227

could for being seen here by the wrong person would shred mine, or rather the Princess's reputation for ever. Who should I go to? Who did I most trust to be alone with? The answer came to mind at once: Bertram. I hurried along to his room, knocked briefly and went in.

There was no one there. Unlike Richenda's Bertram's room was a model of neatness. But his bed too had been slept in. Being left with limited options I went and knocked on Fitzroy's door. He opened it at once. Fitzroy wore a travelling coat. Behind him I could see a valise on the bed. Until this moment I hadn't quite realised how tall he was. He looked down at me and frowned heavily. 'There's no use coming to me now,' he said. 'I told you yesterday to get out of here.' Then he went back into the room and continued to pack. He had left the door open, so I followed him. I even took the dangerous step of closing it behind me.

'You're leaving?'

Fitzroy didn't even both answering this. 'Why now?' I asked.

'Brownly's had a call. He's happy to let me go.' He pulled a draw from the chest and upended it. A cascade of socks fell haphazardly into the valise.

'That's no way to pack!' I said. 'You'll ruin your shirts.'

To my surprise he gave a crack of laughter. 'It's the last thing on my mind,' he said. 'Though I will get the suits sent on. It would be a pity to have to outfit Milford again, as well as expensive.'

'So that isn't who you really are?' I asked.

This won me a genuine smile, 'My dear Euphemia, there are days when even I can barely

228

remember who I am. I am sorry for the trouble that is going to come your way, but I need to remove myself from the situation as quickly as possible.'

'Trouble?' I asked. 'I came to you – well, I tried a few other doors first,' I said with the devastating honesty my father instilled into me, 'but I have seen no one this morning. Not even the maid who should have lit my fire. I have no idea what is going on.'

'Tipton's killed himself,' said Fitzroy as he did a cursory sweep of the room. He locked the valise and turned to face me. 'You had no idea?'

'None,' I said. My voice shook on the single word. 'Are you sure?'

'I know he's dead,' said Fitzroy, 'and I didn't do it. Other than that I have no firm evidence in any direction.'

I moved over and sat down on a chair. 'I can't believe it. Tipton gone.'

'Death has the reputation of being sudden,' said Fitzroy. 'One minute you're here the next you're not. The best any of us can hope for is we go quickly.'

He gave me a pat on the shoulder. 'I hate to be lacking in chivalry, but I need to go and I don't think it's going to help your case if you're found in my room.'

'The police will be asking a lot of questions, won't they?'

'Yes.'

'You think they will discover who I am, don't you?'

'Yes.'

I pressed my fingers to my temples. 'I need time to think.'

'I'm sorry Euphemia. I'm out of here.'

An idea flashed through my brain. 'Take me with you!' I said.

Fitzroy's eyebrows rose. 'Why Euphemia,' he said. 'I didn't know you cared.'

Chapter Thirty-five

Exit of a Princess

'I don't,' I said bluntly. 'I don't want you to take me with you literally. I want you to take the Princess.'

Fitzroy didn't respond, but neither did he walk out the door. I took this an encouragement.

'You said those in the know suspect that you and she were...' I blushed.

'Lovers,' supplied Fitzroy.

'Yes,' I said, 'that. Would it not be likely that if the police had cleared you to leave, you would help her out of this mess for old times' sake?'

'What do you think I might do?' asked Fitzroy, who was by now looking slightly amused.

'Take her away before the questioning began. She can hardly be a suspect. Get her to a train or a boat, so she can return home with no noise or fuss? In fact even suggest to the police that any mention of her here might cause a diplomatic incident?'

'Possible,' said Fitzroy. 'But what in practice do you expect me to do?'

'I'm not sure. I'm still working it out,' I said.

'Give me a plan now or I will have to leave.'

'Right. This might work. Take me with you. People can see me leave. I'll wear a hat with a veil and a long coat.'

'You'd need to. You're a mess,' said Fitzroy.

'Thank you, 'I said. 'You can take me in whatever vehicle you were leaving in anyway to some nearby inn. I'll change back into my housekeeper clothes. Then I'll make my way back here later when there has been time for news to reach me. Richenda has no living relatives. I can say I have come to act as companion for her.'

'Hmm, that could work. I'd have to take you further afield than you think and you'd have to arrive as a housekeeper. That means either you change while we are on the move or in a bush.'

'You could deliver the Princess to a railway station,' I said hopefully. 'I could change in the Ladies' powder room.'

'Alright,' said Fitzroy. 'We'll sort out the final details on route. You will owe me for this. Don't imagine for one moment I won't reclaim this favour.' He picked up his valise. 'I'll come back with you to your room so you can get your coat and hat.'

'I can manage,' I said.

'I have to ensure no one sees you.'

'What if they do?' I asked.

'Then I'll have to kill them.'

'This is no time to joke,' I said angrily. 'A man is dead by his own hand.'

231

'What makes you think I am joking?' said Fitzroy.

I followed him out of the room, well aware I was completely out of my depth. Not that I would let him know this, of course.

What we did, and how I changed from Princess to housekeeper, are not for the pages of this book. I will say Fitzroy was as ruthless efficient as ever and at no time spared my blushes, but he did help me. He even showed me how to darken my hair. Also, I am thankful to say, he did not kill anyone in the process.

Late the next afternoon I arrived at the servants' entrance to the Court. I was neatly dressed, devoid of make-up and the very kind of servant no one would look at twice. Fitzroy had suggested I did my best to stay within the confines of the servants' quarters when I was not attending Richenda and I intended to adhere to his advice. He made me give my word I would not reveal how and with what means we had left. I knew this would anger Rory, but I could see no other way than to accept his rules.

To my great surprise Merry opened the door. She threw her arms around me. 'Thank goodness you're back,' she said half strangling me. 'Rory is being impossible. He's convinced you eloped with Lord Milford.' Then she let go and stood with her hands on her hips. 'I told him not to be so blithering stupid.'

'Thank you.'

'You didn't, did you?'

'No, of course not,' I said incensed. 'I have no

intention of eloping with any one.'

'Well, come on in then and prepare yourself for a frosty reception.'

I followed Merry into the servants' quarters. Before I would have thought them clean and well-lit now, after my time above stairs, they seemed mean and small. The quarters must have been specially built for servants. The ceilings were low and the walls either painted in a dull green or tiled in white. The floors were bare and cold. The lack of colour struck me most.

Merry bustled along a passage way and took me into what I assumed was the butler's pantry. 'Stay 'ere,' she said. 'I'll fetch Rory.'

'Won't Robbins mind me waiting here?' I asked.

Merry stopped. ''Course, you don't know. It was 'im that found Mr Tipton swinging in the music room. Had an 'eart attack.'

'Tipton?'

'No silly. He was already dead. Robbins.'

'Oh my goodness,' I said. 'Did he die?'

'No, but he's right poorly. Rory has been acting a butler.'

'Rory! But surely they had other staff here ready to step into Robbins's shoes?'

'Rory cut down Tipton. Got the doctor sent for. Got Robbins into bed. And generally handled the situation to the Earl's liking.'

'Gosh,' I said, thinking that it might be difficult to marry if we were working in different houses.

'Yeah, I know,' said Merry. 'Some people land on their feet. Won't be a mo.'

I sat down in a chair that must once have graced the upper rooms, but one too many wine stains and a spring that stuck you in an entirely improper place must have relegated it to the servants' quarters. All about me I could hear people moving about their duties. The kitchen must be down here too, but we hadn't passed it on our way in. I began to understand that the servants' quarters here were vast. If Rory took a position here it would be the height of his career.

I gave myself a shake. Here I was thinking only of my romantic life when there had been two deaths in this house and no good answers given. Hopefully, having been on the spot Rory would have some idea of what was occurring.

Almost as if my thoughts had summoned him, Rory appeared in the doorway. He was impressive in the new butler uniform of the Court. He stood in the doorway, unsmiling.

'The uniform suits you,' I said standing.

'Why are you here, Euphemia?' he asked and his voice was colder than I had ever known it.

'Isn't the question rather why did I go?'

'I think we know the answer to that one,' he said. 'Fitzroy. I told you he had his eye on you, but I never thought...'

I took two steps across the floor and slapped him hard on the face. He flinched and put up his hand to touch his reddening cheek.

'How dare you,' I said. 'How dare you, who should know me better than anyone, believe that I would do anything so morally outrageous.'

'You disappeared without a word. What was I supposed to think?'

'I woke up with no servants in sight, the place crawling with police and no one but Milford,

234

Fitzroy, whatever he is calling himself now, on hand to answer my questions.'

'So he suggested that a wee jaunt would be just the thing?'

'No,' I said icily. 'It was my idea.'

'Yours?' said Rory, looking for all the world like the universe was dissolving around him.

'I asked him to help me get the Princess away from here. With two deaths there was little chance that I wouldn't be unmasked. I knew the real Princess and he were supposed to have had an affair, so I thought if he supposedly helped me get away and back to my own country that people would accept it. I never, ever, ever entertained the thought that you would think I had eloped!'

'I see I might have been a wee bit hasty,' said Rory, side stepping to put himself out of my range. 'But you have to think how it looked.'

'It looked how it was meant to look to those upstairs,' I said angrily. 'You knew it was really me. You should have trusted me.'

'Aye well. These have been worrying times. I was ferit for yer. The safest thing I could think o' was for yer to be with yon spy mannie.'

'You're going alarmingly Scotch again,' I said. 'Could it be you are rethinking your position. Might I suggest that an apology might be in order?'

'Aye well. I do think yer could a left me a note. I was out o' my mind with worry, yer ken?'

'So do you still love me?'

'Oh lassie, that was never in question. It's what we do now that's the problem.'

Rory's face fell as he said this last piece. All the

235

anger was gone, but in its place was a look of sorrow. I felt a cold hand clutch at my heart.

But our discussion was rudely broken in on by Merry. 'Sorry! Sorry!' She said, 'But you have to come upstairs and hear what Suzette's got to say. It changes everything.'

Chapter Thirty-six

Tipton's Secret

Merry ran out again at once, so we had no real choice but to follow her. In the corridor Rory leaned in close to speak to me. 'We can't marry,' he said softly. 'Nothing you can say will change that.'

'What? I told you nothing happened with Fitzroy!' I said alarmed and breathless. Merry was setting a furious pace.

'I saw you above stairs. The way you looked, the way you spoke, the way – everything. It's clear you belong with them not me. You should accept Mr Bertram's offer.'

'But I don't want to marry Bertram!'

'He'll give you a far better life than I ever could. My mind's made up.'

'I am not a coat or a hat that can be handed out willy-nilly,' I said angrily. 'I love you. I want to be with you.'

'Sssh,' said Rory, 'let's not be telling everyone our business.'

'We have to discuss this Rory,' I said. 'I don't want to be lady...'

'That doesn't matter. You are one.'

'What are you two whispering about?' said Merry over her shoulder. 'Whatever it is, it will have to wait. Come on!' And she began to clatter up the servants' stair. Conversation was now impossible. I tried to slip my hand into Rory's, but he pulled away.

Merry led the way to the small study where I had been interviewed by the police. She threw the door open dramatically to reveal Suzette, Richard and Bertram! The expression on her face told us she had not been expecting this welcoming committee.

'Ah, I heard you were back,' said Richard. 'I'm not sure why you thought it was necessary, but it will save me a trip.'

Bertram gave his half-brother a quizzical glance, but came forward to greet me warmly. 'I am very glad to see you safe and well.' he said. 'Suzette, my late mother's maid, has courageously made a full statement to the police and it clears matters up completely.'

'What? What on earth could she have said to do that?'

Suzette sneered slightly. 'I told them as how I knew Mr Tipton from before. Cos he didn't use his actual name. Had a nickname like most of the clients. Fitted him nice I thought it did. It was...'

Bertram put up his hand to stop her. 'I don't think we need to go into the details again, Suzette. Suffice it to say. Euphemia, that Suzette knew something very much to Tipton's detriment. She

237

told my mother, who tried to warn Richenda, who angrily rejected the news. Obviously, Tipton was afraid that with time Lady Stapleford would convince her, or perhaps Richard or myself, so he decided there was only one way to silence her. Later, when Suzette came forward with her evidence he must have realised that he would be caught and took his own life.'

'You were blackmailing him when I saw you together in the garden,' I said.

'I was not,' said Suzette angrily. 'I was telling him to give himself up.'

'But I saw him give you money,' I said.

'You little snip...' started Suzette, then she glanced over at Richard. 'He was giving me a letter to give to Richenda to explain everything, but it was so unpleasant I burnt it.'

Richard nodded approvingly. 'My sister should never have heard of this matter.'

'Bertram,' I said as calmly as I could, for it was being a most trying day, 'will you please explain what Tipton's great secret was.'

'He had syphilis,' blurted out Merry and then clapped her hand over her mouth.

'That would explain why he had been acting so oddly lately,' said Rory. 'In the final stages I hear men go mad.'

'I'm afraid so,' said Bertram. 'Uncontrollable and violent rages. It explains many of his previous actions,' he said added emphasis to the last words and I knew he was thinking of Mrs Wilson.

'But this doesn't make any sense,' I said. 'How did Lady Stapleford know?'

'Cos I told her,' said Suzette. 'She ain't very

238

bright, is she?'

'But how...?' Then an image came to my mind, the very one I'd be searching for a long time, Suzette's face the first time she saw Tipton. She'd been travelling with Lady Stapleford and had refused to eat her meals with the Stapleford Hall staff. The first time she had laid eyes on Tipton had been that time in my room, when I had seen her go white from shock. 'You knew him from before, didn't you?'

'Might have done,' said Suzette. 'Certainly heard of him and his doings.'

'Yes, you are one of my successes, aren't you?' said a voice from the doorway. It was Richenda, dressed in full black and looking like a thunder-cloud. 'Those centres Daddy hated me setting up and working with. You remember, Euphemia?'

'But that means Suzette used to be a whore!' said Merry. As soon as she had said this she clapped both hands over the mouth.

'I was a gentleman's companion,' said Suzette, 'though never his. But I heard how he had it. There are signs.'

'Enough,' said Bertram. 'We don't need to sully the ladies' ears with any more sordid details.'

Suzette shrugged. 'Seems to me the ladies are better knowing what to look out for.' I silently thought she had a point.

'Enough,' said Rory loudly. 'I'll no have the like of you in this house.'

'Oh, I'm off alright,' said Suzette. 'Going to set meself up as a milliner. Might sell you an 'at one day ladies. I'll give you a discount!' And with that she left the room, her nose high in the air.

'Thank goodness that's over,' said Bertram. 'Merry, I'm surprised at you.'

'Sorry, sir. It was the shock, sir.'

'Yes, well, now we can put all this nastiness behind us.'

'Did you tell Tipton what Suzette had told Lady Stapleford?' I asked Richenda.

'I did not,' said Richenda firmly. 'I didn't believe a word of it and I wasn't going to let anyone spoil my day.'

'So Tipton had no reason to kill Lady Stapleford?'

'You said yourself Suzette was blackmailing him,' said Bertram.

'It doesn't feel right,' I said. 'I saw that after Lady Stapleford was killed. If she thought he was a killer would she have risked blackmail? And how did he know in the first place?'

'The girl must have gone to him first,' said Bertram.

'Then why didn't he just kill her?' said Rory. 'Far easier to get the police to overlook the death of a maid of dubious background than a lady. Instead of which he gave her money afterwards. That's not the action of a killer.'

'He wasn't in his right mind,' said Bertram. 'We have to make allowance for that.'

'He did not kill Stepmama,' said Richenda stoutly.

'Listen, all of you,' boomed Richard suddenly, 'I have had enough of this gossip and unpleasantness. The police have closed the case and I have paid Suzette a tidy sum so she doesn't spread rumours about the kind of man my sister was pre-

240

pared to marry.'

'You take that back, Richard,' said his sister.

'Moreover, as all those involved are present here, I think it is time to announce some changes. Euphemia St John, I hereby give you notice that your services are no longer required. I will not have my household disrupted by your foolish and headstrong ideas any longer. Any foolish attempts to spread rumours about myself or my family will be met with my word of the unsavouriness of your character and your propensity to throw yourself at the men around you.' Any case that I might have made was somewhat undermined by both Bertram and Rory shouting in my defence.

'Merry,' said Richard, raising his voice about theirs, 'as chief maid, will suffice to head the female staff as I am shutting up Stapleford Hall to be in town, while Rory is lent to the Earl to head up his staff.'

'You never said I was to replace Euphemia,' wailed Merry. 'You only said I would be head maid.'

'As my brother currently does not have a household, his property, as I understand it, being mostly under the Fens, you are now a person of no abode and no position, Euphemia, and as such I must ask you to vacate this house.'

I felt nothing; no anger, only shock that it would end this way with Richard winning. I had no doubt in my mind that he had killed Lady Stapleford and arranged Tipton's so-called suicide. As I looked into his eyes, I shivered: here was a man who was getting a liking for killing. But who would ever believe me?

241

'Of course, anyone who continues to associate with Euphemia will have no place on my staff or in my home.' He came towards his sister. 'I am planning on hiring a place in the city for a while. There, my dear sister, I hope you will be able to forget this sordid episode and move on with your life.'

'That's what is to happen to me, is it?' said Richenda. 'You've decided none of us will stay at Stapleford Hall – you've decided...' She inhaled deeply, gritted her teeth, and said, 'Can you get it through your thick head, Richard, that you do not control either Bertram or me. We have every right to stay at the Hall if we wish.'

Bertram, who had been standing with his mouth hanging open, rather like a fish that has just been told fishermen exist, said, 'I don't want to be there.'

'Yes, I imagine I have just rid the place of one of its primary attractions for you,' sneered Richard.

'Richard,' said Richenda, and this time her voice snapped like a whip, 'do not think for one moment I believe any of the lies you have told here. As for throwing Euphemia out, let me tell you: she has a new position with me. She will be my companion.'

'What do you need one of them for?' laughed Richard.

'Because,' said Richenda, 'I am going to stay with the Muller family while I recover from this tragedy. You remember the Mullers? Your main banking rivals? This is my little birthday present to myself. Had you forgotten, dear brother, it's our birthday today, and while I may have no

242

husband I finally have my inheritance. Come, Euphemia! We have much to discuss!'

Bertram was still speechless. Rory couldn't look me in the eye and Merry was crying silently. Richard had done his best to strip me of my allies, and in so doing had made me his sister's best weapon. I trusted Richenda no further than I could throw her (which wouldn't be very far, for as I have said she is rather a large lady), but now she was all that stood between my family and my destitution. With tears in my eyes, I took one final look at my old friends, standing powerless before my worst enemy, and then I turned and followed Richenda silently from the room.

I did not look back.

Epilogue

I know that in my writings I have often amused my readers both intentionally and unintentionally. I feel guilty for ending this story on such a sour note, but it was a terrible time in my life and the effects of these murders changed many lives. However, it is not the end of my story nor the end of my fight. You can read about my next adventure…

Fingal County Libraries

The publishers hope that this book has given you enjoyable reading. Large Print Books are especially designed to be as easy to see and hold as possible. If you wish a complete list of our books please ask at your local library or write directly to:

Magna Large Print Books
Magna House, Long Preston,
Skipton, North Yorkshire.
BD23 4ND

This Large Print Book for the partially sighted, who cannot read normal print, is published under the auspices of

THE ULVERSCROFT FOUNDATION

THE ULVERSCROFT FOUNDATION

... we hope that you have enjoyed this Large Print Book. Please think for a moment about those people who have worse eyesight problems than you ... and are unable to even read or enjoy Large Print, without great difficulty.

You can help them by sending a donation, large or small to:

**The Ulverscroft Foundation,
1, The Green, Bradgate Road,
Anstey, Leicestershire, LE7 7FU,
England.**
or request a copy of our brochure for more details.

The Foundation will use all your help to assist those people who are handicapped by various sight problems and need special attention.

Thank you very much for your help.